THE MOST BEAUTIFUL INSANITY

by Heather Wilde

D0863204

For Milana

Published in the United States of America by Palm Circle Press

Cover Photo by Rodolfo Clix

Cover Design by Alam Twaha

"Beauty can be as isolating as genius, or de-formity. I have always been aware of a relation-ship between madness and beauty."

— Richard Avedon

1

Drexel Waters was having sex with her from behind. The Ecstasy pill kicked in as he came, and it was Heaven. The most intense orgasm of all time. And all this despite not being able to see her, not even a shape. (The closet light didn't work.) But there was something extra sensual about this, sex without sight, only the feel of her hips, the slightness of her waist, her pleased whimpering.

Over a year ago they'd been in a photoshoot together, a *BodyQuake* cologne ad. She'd sat topless in his lap with her nipples blocked from view by her own strategically placed arm. In the picture, she pressed her nose bridge against his temple, an off-camera, blue light giving their torsos millions of glimmering, blue sweat beads. They were now at a New Year's Eve street party, three blocks cordoned off with barricades. People packed the lobbies of two neighboring hotels the colors of cake frosting. More people overflowed between them.

When he'd first seen her from across the lobby, he hadn't recognized her, only knew that she looked familiar. She'd dyed her hair blond, cut it some. Drexel approached her, though not until Ophelia, his girlfriend, spotted a distant knot of friends and squealed over to them.

There was the question of familiarity, then recognition and surprise, then—a utility closet in the lobby. He couldn't recount the exact steps other than that. He no longer even noticed how he got himself into these situations anymore: sex in bathrooms, sex behind bushes, sex in parks, sex on the beach, sex with this face, sex with that face; yet he was not unaware, not unappreciative, of how many other men would love to be him, would sell their *souls* for it. He would, too, if he wasn't him. But fuck it, he was. Drexel Waters, Male Fashion Model, Pussy Magnet.

"Yeah," the girl gasped. "Inside me, yeah."

Drexel withdrew his penis from her and slapped her ass. He zipped up, laughing. Life was too much. He stumbled out of the closet, into the hallway, and found himself within a circle of people—an audience, no doubt, drawn by her pleasured noises. He made a quick scan for Ophelia among the giggling people but was lucky this time. Rushing from the Ecstasy, the newest conquest, he pulled the girl out behind him while she fought her skirt down. He raised their hands into the air, victorious. Drexel Waters howled.

Ophelia felt herself lifted by Drexel, folded over his shoulder. Camera flashes went off as she pounded his back with her fists, laughing, saying, "Let me down, let me down! *Drexel!*" When he let her down, she locked her arms around his neck and hung there.

Ophelia had dressed for the occasion in a silver, mylar slip dress with string-laced, six-inch heels of death, her hair piled into a loose mound. Drexel wore black dungarees with a black long sleeve, cotton shirt, the number 666 in red across the chest and twice more down each sleeve.

Bass-heavy dance music pulsed from tripod-supported speakers. In the center of the street sat a carnival tent; a runway extended from its entrance like a lit tongue. Male and female models, wearing elaborately pointy outfits, paraded to the runway's end before pausing there to do something brash and unexpected, such as moon the crowd or grab their crotch. Though the entire stage area was strobed by camera flashes, no one in the street paid much attention. Most danced or gathered into conversational clusters.

Ophelia caught Drexel's eyes wandering the lobby.

"Who are you looking for?" she asked, regaining her feet.

"Mind your business. Give me those drugs."

She dug into her purse and removed a tiny baggie puffed with white powder. She handed it to him, forgoing covertness. He didn't seem to notice. No one did.

On the far side of the lobby, people began shouting a countdown which spread through the room. At countdown's end, everyone erupted into celebratory wails and whistles and they jumped up and down. They created a blizzard of white and blue confetti, webbed each other in fluorescent silly string.

Ophelia punched his arm. "You going to kiss me or hug me or something?"

He looked at her, puzzled. "Why?" His face went slack. "Oh, yeah. Happy New Year."

She turned to walk away, but he caught her elbow. "Hey, where you going? I'm not ready to leave."

"Just fuck you, okay?" she said, talking over him. "I'm leaving now so you can finish having fun. Sorry I interrupted."

"Ophelia, hon, are you sure it was *Ecstasy* you took?"

She tugged her arm free and walked away. She thought she was headed towards the exit but somehow got turned around. She entered the courtyard instead. She lit a cigarette behind a potted palm tree and searched the crowd for anyone she might know. She watched a beautiful woman in an epidermal black dress arguing loudly with her date...a semi-circle of people speaking in a language she'd never heard before...a larger group of people being entertained by a magician, his tricks involving a red handkerchief which disappeared and reappeared from one gloved hand to another.

She didn't know any of these people. Not one single soul. After a tentative look around her, making sure she'd lost Drexel, she took one of the palm tree's blades in her fingers. Ophelia examined the blade as if it were the most interesting thing she'd ever seen and tried not to cry. She took her phone out of her purse and called her other boyfriend.

Drexel found the girl from the closet again and went with her to her hotel room, one flight upstairs from the party. He sat with his knees on the floor as he worked over the bed, dividing the drug into lines with his Visa card. She had volunteered, as a work surface, a vinyl binder with ALLISON TAYLOR, INC. stamped on its cover. Her portfolio book.

The drug resembled cocaine, but it wasn't cocaine.

"What, you do this stuff like cocaine?" Drexel asked her.

The girl leaned forward on the bed, sitting with her legs drawn beneath her. "Yeah, you snort it, dummy," she said.

Her eyes closed and her lids fluttered, trance-like. She smiled. Her lids withdrew over wet, red eyes. They looked at each other. Music and voices from downstairs percolated up through the floor. A car alarm wailed two times from the street, its third note cut off in mid-chirp.

"So which agency you with?" he asked her. He placed a twenty-dollar bill beneath his nose and leaned down to the bed. He inhaled a line with his right nostril, tapped its side to help it all up there. He handed her the twenty and her portfolio.

She sat back, balanced the book in one hand, held the twenty with the other. She inhaled a line by running the end of the rolled bill along the book's length. She leaned away and pinched her nostrils together. She pressed her eyes shut.

"*Ouch*," she said. "My nose. God. Hurts, right?"

Like he'd snorted *Tabasco Sauce*. But he motioned for the portfolio back anyway. Already, there was a new sensation expanding through his skin. Hot air seeped from his pores. He felt helium-headed. "Is it supposed to hurt?" he asked her.

She held her hand out for her portfolio. Accepting the

book back, she set it on the bed and looked at him. "Mmmm, I love, love, *love* drugs," she said in a dream-slow voice. "Feel anything?"

"Like my heart's going to explode out of my chest. Like... like..." He laughed, and she laughed too, and their laughter built on top of each other, fed by the fact that they were laughing for no apparent reason.

The girl slid onto her stomach and moved her bent legs back and forth behind her. She whited her thumb from a leftover drug smudge, then kissed her thumb clean. "Hey! The infamous Drexel Waters is in my room. Right on."

He chopped together more lines. "Your name's Heather, right?"

She blew a laugh, fluttering her lips. "Holly."

"Where you from, Holly?"

"My mother." She rolled over and stood on the back of her neck. She balanced her body straight up into the air with her hands supporting her sides.

"Damn, look at you," he said.

She pedaled her legs. "Yeah, I used to be a gymnast. A dancer, too. I love dancing more than anything."

"A dancer? Like a stripper?"

"The ballet! Are you being serious right now?"

"Never."

"My dad paid for lessons. He pays for everything. You've probably even heard of him. Gary Nash?"

"Who?"

"Never mind."

"He an actor?"

"Don't you watch television? The news? Nothing?"

"Who is he?"

"No, you've never heard of him. I prefer it that way. Wait, did you actually say '*stripper*?'"

Drexel set the portfolio topped with drugs on the floor. He took a hotel pen from the nightstand before lying on the bed next to her. He held her arm in his hand and began drawing on her skin.

She lifted her arm to see. "What are you doing?"

"Be still."

"What are you drawing?"

"Something."

"Ow! Not so hard. I want to draw on you."

He leaned up and grabbed the other pen from atop the hotel stationary. He gave it to her. She uncapped the lid and stared at his sleeved bicep, the 666 there.

Drexel drew a dragon on the under part of her arm. The drawing started with the dragon's tail at the palm of her hand, going all the way to below her armpit where the last flaming crescent of dragon breath ended.

When he was done, she turned her arm sideways to see the drawing. "What is that, the Loch Ness Monster? You didn't sign it." She offered her arm back.

Drexel instead printed his name with his hotel's phone number beneath. It was the safest means of contact since Ophelia was always going through his phone. "That's a dragon," he said. He looked at his own arm. "I thought you were going to draw something on *me*."

"I couldn't think of anything. Let me up." She patted his head. "I need a shower before I pass out or...Cool, I'll bet the water's going to feel *trippy*."

"But you'll wash my name and phone number away. Dude, you'll need that later."

"I won't wash this arm then. Ever again. Come on. Up, up, up. I'll be right out."

He moved over and watched her get to her feet, stagger into the bathroom. He heard the squeal of the faucets being turned, the released water hissing through the shower nozzle. She'd left the door open. Was this a hint she wanted him to join her? Is this why she mentioned the way the water might feel? He heard the rhythm of the falling water become muffled, as she must have been stepping beneath it.

Drexel decided to follow her, but his body wouldn't obey

his brain's command for movement. He looked at his feet and marveled at how far away they were. He wiggled his toes and they multiplied. He hadn't been the least bit aware this drug caused hallucinations. Was pretty sure it wasn't supposed to. Shit was off.

The bathroom door opened wide and the girl named Holly was standing there, burritoed by a white bath towel, her skin ruddy from the shower's heat. Her wet hair hung in dark strands over her face. She bunched up her hair with one hand, grinned. She dropped the towel.

He stared at her body. Not bad, though he'd never been a big fan of pubic region tattoos. Why decorate something already so beautiful? Thankfully, her tattoo was tiny. A ladybug.

"Let's fuck again?" she asked him. "With the lights this time?"

Drexel was on the verge of complying when it occurred to him, feeling so removed from his body, an erection might be work. Holly began to walk towards him, but he waved her to a halt. "Dance for me," he said.

"Now? Naked? You wish."

He lay across the bed with his hand cradling his head. "Don't be chicken. Show me some ballet."

She closed her eyes and shook her arms out. She cleared her throat, twisted slightly from the waist and stumbled, almost toppling. She caught herself against the wall. Drexel went to laugh but saw that she wasn't. She made a fist and pressed the palm side to her forehead.

"I haven't danced...ballet...in...ohmygod...soooooo loooong." She dropped her arm. She looked at the floor, her face clouding. A minute went by.

"What's up? You cool?" he asked her. "You're not O.D.'ing on me, are you?"

She placed a finger against her lips and took two trembling steps away from the wall. "Shhhhh...Okay, here we go. I'm dancing."

Holly stood with one foot on tiptoes, bringing the other

leg up and pointing it horizontally. She curled her arms away from her body at the twelve and four o'clock positions. She pivoted, but sunk slowly, slowly to the floor, like she'd simply chosen this moment to take a nap.

Using his elbows, Drexel snaked across the bed to see her. She lay there in a pretzeled heap.

"No, you don't," he said. "Don't do that. No, no, no. Please, don't do that...Ah, fuck!"

The floor stretched away from him. She stretched away. Or Drexel himself stretched away. Everything stretched away.

He reached to wake her, and his arm wiggled down the canyon wall of her bed. With two fingers, he pressed hard against her shoulder blade. Transfixed with the pliability of her skin, he massaged it, played the piano on it. Some minutes later, she hadn't stirred. He got off the bed, knelt next to her. He turned her over. Her lips and chin were oiled with clear vomit. He felt her neck and wrists for a pulse. He felt nothing but wasn't sure he was even doing it right. He placed an ear against her chest—still nothing. He stood and continued staring at her and, again, extended until he was miles above her.

He decided to find someone who could do something about this. A person was dying here. Experts were needed.

"Dammit." He repeated the word until it became a chant beneath his breath. "Dammit, dammit, dammit..."

He stepped to the front door and opened it. He faded through the hallway's floor and landed into a crouch next to a bar. He struggled to his feet and found himself standing beside a nine-foot-tall drag queen. She wore a rainbow headdress of fluffy boas, scraping the floor behind her. The drag queen seemed to know him.

"*There* you are," she said. "I saw Ophelia leave. She go home?"

Drexel leaned against the bar and crossed his legs. "Yes... Ophelia. I worship the dirt she treats me like. And blah and blah and blah, blah, you know?"

The queen placed a hand on his neck and gave it a light

shake. "You all right? Your eyes are like golf balls."

Drexel shook his head.

"Ha! Your fly's open!" she said, overjoyed.

Drexel backed away from her. He needed new air. He remembered an entrance somewhere off to the left. Through a foreground of smoking, drinking heads, he saw a large rectangle of smeared, moist light, growing brighter.

His brow met the floor before his nose did and his sight went yellow. He heard people call his name. He heard someone yell, "Oh, *yeah*, baby! Another one bites the dust! *Whoooooo! Whoooooo!*" And he heard the eighteen-year-old girl named Holly asking him what was taking so long.

That girl! She needed help for some reason. Yes, he remembered now. He was looking for help. They needed help.

Drexel Waters lost consciousness and the room became lit by camera flashes, busy and bright as fireworks. It was a new year.

2

"It's a miraculous world," said the man on TV. He was overlooking the smoky-violet distance of a canyon.

Trace watched from his chair, sunk low with his legs crossed, a Jack bottle balanced with a hand atop his lap. He watched the commercial with the same bored patience he did for all of TV. Didn't care what it said or did as long as it didn't make him think too much about it.

The wind outside manipulated the window blinds behind him, making them quiver with a sound like rattlesnakes. The wind pushed in the smell of tropical plants, blossoming in January somehow, along with the stench of upset dumpsters. There was the panicked palpitation of salsa music from an apartment building nearby, maybe his own. He couldn't tell. Didn't care much. Every now and then came the distant pop and sizzle of firecrackers.

"One little pill makes all your discomfort go away," said the woman standing next to the man who overlooked the smoky-violet distance of a canyon.

"Wouldn't you like this to be you?" asked a voice over.

Surely, Trace thought. He set the bottle on the floor and promised himself he wouldn't take another sip. He'd had enough, thank you. Weird thoughts were sneaking up on him—

harmful thoughts: his ex-fiancée, his father, his ex-fiancée again, the dead and maimed always more present in their absence during the holidays. He reached his socked foot out until his big toe was against the TV screen. He touched the nose of a laughing blond woman riding a horse, followed her with his toe, even after she'd galloped off-screen. His foot fell from the side of the TV and hit the floor.

"What is that?" the TV asked.

"That," the TV answered itself, "is a bar of soap."

Trace had never felt so lonely in his life.

His phone trilled. Trace looked at it on the third ring, walked over and answered it by the fifth. It was Enrique, his partner, calling to wish him a "Happy New Year." And to ask for a big, big favor. Trace turned down the TV to hear him. What kind of favor?

"There's been a Section 32 on First and Ocean."

Trace exhaled. "And?"

"Oh God, please, Trace. I told you what I had planned for tonight. I'm with that girl! It's New Year's Eve!"

"You're right in the middle of things," Trace offered.

"The *utter* middle of things. Besides, you live closer."

"A Section 32 though? That's not our department."

"Well, they're asking for Homicide for some reason. One of us has to go."

"There's no one else who can? Not one person?" Trace sat on the arm of his couch. "I'm sick. You *know* I'm sick." As if to validate this, he snorted wetly and coughed.

"Trace, it'll take you thirty minutes. Metro has probably done most of the work already. All you'll have to do is make an appearance. In, out, zip, over."

Trace stood and stretched, making sure he groaned with it. "I don't know," he said.

"Thirty minutes, big guy. I'll owe you a drink. *Two* drinks. Swear on my mother's grave."

Trace visored his forehead with his hand and squeezed his temples. "Make it three drinks. Because I'm planning to stay pissed about this for a while."

A female voice on Enrique's end mumbled something and the voice and Enrique laughed.

"Enrique?"

"Yeah, yeah. I swear," Enrique said, still expelling hiccups of laughter. "Three drinks."

Trace hung up the phone and stood looking at the TV. The horizontal dial had fallen out of adjustment and the picture rolled. Still, he could make out a black & white shot of several silhouetted soldiers raising an American flag, as if into a great wind. The picture switched to a test pattern before collapsing into snow.

He stumbled into his bedroom and dressed, trying to re-member where he'd parked his car last. He was more or less sure he remembered. He looked fifteen minutes for his 9mm Glock before realizing he'd left it in its shoulder holster, which he found in his closet. It wasn't until he was in his white Toyota 4Runner (bought used four months ago) and halfway to where he was going that he remembered his badge. It was still in his wallet on the bedroom floor. He'd seen it, told himself to pick it up, but forgot.

Trace pounded the steering wheel with the heel of his left hand. "Fuck me! Fuck!" he bellowed. He stewed for a moment, yelled "fuck" again, and was silent.

There was one thing for sure: This was not going to be some thirty-minute in and out like Enrique had guaranteed. It was New Year's Eve—or *New Year's*, Trace guessed it had to be by now—and such a holiday always turned South Miami Beach into a gridded peninsula of bumper-to-bumper traffic. The blue siren on Trace's dash was useless. Cars wouldn't get out of his way be-cause there was nowhere to get out of his way *to*. Each street was six different kinds of crammed.

Trace used a breathing method he remembered from Yoga class. His ex-fiancée, Cassie, had talked him into going once. Breathe in through the nose, using the stomach, breathe out through the mouth, using the chest. This helped him concentrate, something he needed now to keep him from, say, not applying the brakes in time and plowing into someone's rear. Doubting his blood-alcohol level was anywhere near legal, Trace understood that a collision, no matter how minor, would send numerous matters to Hell. Perhaps this was what he wanted. Needed even. Go ahead and bottom-out already.

When he arrived at the scene, he parked sideways across the street, alongside three parked squad cars and an ambulance. The neighborhood twirled within a spinning color show of siren lights.

Four short tugs on a flask. One more. Another. A last long one and Trace was ready for this. Walking past the barricades, through the street party, he felt assaulted by music, an electro-beat echoing from every direction. He felt stunned this many people could mill around a tragedy and still require a sound-track for it. This wasn't the scene Trace had expected. An over-dose scene, even on South Beach, normally involved a squalid, isolated setting, not a celebrative, crowded one.

The first officer Trace saw was Carlos Gutierrez, coming out of the nearest hotel. Thank God. It didn't matter now that Trace had forgotten his badge. He'd known Carlos for...ten, eleven years? Trace even suspected Carlos for carrying a kind of subdued adulation for him. Most city cops, Trace was convinced, owned aspirations of becoming homicide detectives. And why wouldn't they? You got to wear a decent suit and carry your badge in your wallet and you didn't have to drive a conspicuous squad car. No more domestic disputes, no more fender benders.

Still, Carlos nearly walked by Trace without seeing him. Didn't stop until Trace patted his arm.

"Merry Fucking Christmas," Trace said. "'New Year's,' I mean."

"Trace, you're here. Where's Enrique?"

"Out on the town. Being Enrique."

Carlos laughed.

Nearby, two paramedics pushed a stretcher through the

hotel's entrance. On the stretcher lay a human-shaped mound, shrouded by a dark-pink polypropylene sheet. Carlos waved for the paramedics to stop.

"You're not going to believe who this is," Carlos said to Trace while walking him to the stretcher. "She was found naked." He lifted a corner of the sheet. "Look at the body she had."

"I should recognize her?" Trace unfolded a handkerchief from his coat pocket and blew his nose.

Though Carlos lifted the sheet further, revealing more of the girl, Trace remained focused on her face. It held the expression of the typical heart attack victim: raised brows, ovaled mouth, eyes questioning though sightless, surprised to be dead. Trace wasn't accustomed to seeing this expression on anyone younger than fifty. This girl looked barely sixteen. His gaze wandered from her face to her smallish breasts, periscoped flat, to the pelvis bones bracketing her thighs, to the tiny ladybug tattoo above her pubic hair. No bruises anywhere. Not one.

Carlos laughed gamely. "What a waste. Did you see her arm?"

"Her arm?"

"Look at her arm."

Trace spotted a second tattoo filling the girl's inner arm. Embarrassing that he could have missed it—the tat was huge.

He turned the limb outward for a better look. It wasn't a tattoo. It was sweat-smudged. It was a pen drawing of...a monster? A dinosaur? He leaned in, squinting. It was breathing fire. A dragon. There was something else too, written across the dragon's belly: DREXEL 622-8200 RM 202.

Trace knew that name. Was fairly certain he even knew the handwriting. "You called this phone number, right?" he asked.

"About fifty times. No one answers his room. The phone number belongs to The Wave Hotel, five blocks from here on Washington. His full name's 'Drexel Waters.' Guy's already on probation for a statutory rape charge."

"And he's a male fashion model."

"How'd you know?"

Christ, it *was* him. Anyway, this had Drexel's calamitous vibe all over it. "I guess maybe I've heard of the guy," Trace said, cringing, praying Carlos wouldn't follow up with more questions. "Has anyone gone to his hotel?"

"Yeah, but front desk hasn't seen him yet. We left a message."

"A message." Trace stepped aside when he noticed the paramedics impatiently watching them, awaiting some sign, any sign that it was okay for them to continue.

The paramedics wheeled the stretcher down the lane of celebrants which had formed, starting from the sidewalk to the ambulance's rear. Their rushed speech made Trace think of turkeys. Many of them were actually smiling, probably already constructing the incident into its retelling. They had come here tonight to rejoice in the end of the year, the beginning of another. It was supposed to be a night for closure and restoration and a corpse had gone and shown up. That girl right there was d-e-a-d.

"The girl was a model, too," Carlos said. "From New York. Here's the fun part. Ready? Heard of Gary Nash? Big real estate guy?"

"No."

"Gets interviewed on MSN a lot? Anyway, that's his daughter we just saw dead and naked. This is going to be bigger news than..." Carlos trailed off, at a loss for a good metaphor. "We'll be getting our names in the paper."

"What was the girl's name?"

Carlos had to check a notepad: "Holly Nash, eighteen-years old. Roommate found her around 3:30, about ten minutes after people saw this Drexel character leave the same room, running like a deer."

The radio on Carlos' hip came to life with amplified, pinch-nosed chatter. He brought the radio to his mouth, said something back, replaced it. "The last anyone saw of Drexel

Waters, he was getting into a cab."

The crowd lost its shape as it broke into thinner bands. The ambulance nudged its way through the street, siren lights rhythmically illuminating a stockinged leg, a blink of sequin.

Trace blew his nose again, honking it strong. "Was it heroin?"

"Lab just left actually. M.E.'s vol/tox said it's methamphetamine. Purest stuff he's ever seen. The roommate told us that before Holly Nash went upstairs, she bumped into her and asked her if she wanted to join them. Said she'd met *the* Drexel Waters and he'd invited them to 'go back to their room to go flying.' But the roommate wasn't interested."

Trace rubbed his forehead to clear the warm fuzziness from his brain. "Carlos, so...you want to bust this guy for parole violation? Sharing his drugs? Have fun. This isn't a homicide."

"The girl started dying and the guy split instead of helping her. Law calls that 'a total disregard for human life,' Trace. That's a *type* of murder, no?"

"Was anyone else in the room?"

"Doesn't look like it. Not so far."

"Still possible that he left the room before anything even happened. Could've been running away because he was late for somewhere. Who knows? I'll bet that not one of the witnesses you spoke to could claim sobriety."

"Even so, her father hangs out with the Bush family and the Clintons and those people. You're going to have to come up with *something* so this isn't his daughter's own fault. Watch."

"And we're positive it's an overdose?"

"M.E. believes it. Drug's all over the room, in her nose. Besides, I looked her over myself. No bruises, no strangulation marks, *nada.*"

Carlos' radio hissed, and he raised it again to his mouth. "Q.S.L.," he said. He placed the radio back. He pointed up and behind himself. "The room is on the second floor. Did you want to look it over?"

"Surely."

Trace followed Carlos into the lobby. As they ascended the stairs, Carlos nudged Trace and asked him if he'd been having a good time tonight. Trace said he was sick with a cold; he'd been sleeping. Carlos laughed and said he didn't *smell* too much like he'd only been sleeping. Carlos made several broad waves with his hand beneath his nose, fanning away Trace's alcoholic vapor.

On the halfway landing of the stairs, Trace was afforded an overview of the lobby. It had been emptied of people but remained coated in confetti and silly string. Helium balloons huddled together on the ceiling, orphaned, their spiraled ribbons dangling like rainbow-colored moss.

3

Sixty yards from shore, Ophelia sat in a canvas chair with her legs in the seat, the bottoms of her feet pressed together. The wind off the ocean made her warmer than she already was.

"How much did you sleep last night?" asked the makeup artist—a plump twenty-something girl with blood-bright lipstick to match her blood-bright jumpsuit.

Ophelia told the truth. She was so exhausted, it didn't occur to her to do otherwise. "An hour maybe," she said. "I'll be fine. "

The makeup artist sighed all her breath away. She rushed an applicator over a dish of burnt-sienna eyeshadow. "You girls make this utterly impossible for me. I wish you could know. Or give a shit."

Ophelia decided not to say anything, just deal with it. Having lost too many days to rain, shooting on New Year's Day had become necessary and everyone was in a sour mood over it. No energy for conflict anyway. She'd slept so little herself because she'd spent most of the night arguing with Drexel. She replayed his words for a denial, but he hadn't denied anything. He never did. And, in a way, he never had to. Hints of his infidelities were anywhere she wanted to look—the faint aroma of some other girl's pussy on his fingers, his annoyed reaction to questions concerning where he'd been for a week, the impossible swiftness with which "they" finished a box of condoms. What other evidence did she need?

In retaliation, she'd bought a bottle of aconite online a month ago. She'd sprinkled a little into the crystal meth before giving it to Drexel last night. Aconite was a plant that was commonly made into skin cream, a fact she became familiar with while working a photo shoot, an editorial for a major skincare company. They were marketing the stuff as their next miracle product. Problem was, while topically beneficial, ingesting aconite could be dangerous. Was even labeled "the perfect murder weapon" since it was so hard to find in most any autopsy. Not that she'd intended to kill Drexel, of course, only make him sick. Or maybe she *did* want him dead. Either way, it was a crazy thing to have done because he was driving her fucking crazy.

Of course, Ophelia herself enjoyed the occasional side relationship but that was another Ophelia, the one living inside of her, a far more vengeful and impulsive person. Her secret affairs were rare anyway. They meant nothing to her and she never thought about them. If she didn't think about them, they didn't exist.

Meanwhile Drexel continued to live, even had the balls to show up at her hotel that morning, wanting to crawl into bed with her, begging her, saying he needed to cuddle. With her. Was dying for it. And, as usual, she'd been too disoriented and drained to resist him. Ophelia felt increasingly light-headed now, thinking about it. She closed her eyes and decided to let the droning symphony of the beach wash her mind away. She listened to a whirring motorboat, the respiration of waves, the wavering tone of other human voices...

"How many times have I redone you? Seven?" the makeup artist asked her. "Look at you. You've got circles beneath your eyes, pimples. And they want me to fix you in five minutes? *Sheeyah*, right."

A palm frond hissing, bothered with wind, the respiration of nearby traffic..."And there's not even twenty minutes of sunlight left. What am I, a magician? Ala-kazam?"

A car horn, the overhead murmur of an airplane, yelping laughter of seagulls...

"And if this shot has to be postponed," the makeup artist wanted to know, "whose fault will it be? I'll give you a hint: not yours."

Ophelia passed out. Her head dropped. Inwardly sensing the inappropriateness of losing consciousness right then, she jolted awake. But not before the makeup artist's applicator stabbed a burnt-sienna comet down Ophelia's cheek.

"Oh, wonderful. Thank you," the makeup artist said. "You're a real superstar. Can I have your autograph?"

A bulk of white wedding train swirled around and behind her, held down in places by unseen rocks. Also unseen were the clips and pins and tape pulling the wedding dress tight in back, giving the illusion that the dress fit perfectly. Beyond her, the sun descended a ladder of clouds, almost to the horizon, sending off an atomic explosion of sunlight.

Ophelia could feel herself slipping, gravity winning the tug. She stood at a slightly sloping angle on a boulder, one among hundreds forming a peninsula in the hazel surf, calm as pond water. It was the heels. They were causing her to slide. The angle of where she stood put too much pressure on her toes.

She felt increasingly woozy, as though a sickness inside of her were spreading by the second. She wondered if she might fall to her death but didn't dare move. There wasn't time. The light was leaving.

The photographer stood over his tripod, thirty yards away, looking through the camera's Birdseye. "Dearie, for chrissakes, hold the veil higher!" he called in a British accent, sharp enough to cut a hole through cement. "Keep the bloody thing up!"

Ophelia held the veil higher. A little more. *Hurry, hurry,*

hurry, she thought. She felt herself slipping faster. *Jesus Christ, hurry!*

"And smile for me dammit!" the photographer yelled. "You're supposed to be happy, dear! Happy! That's your wedding dress! You're getting *married*! All of your dreams are coming true! Now smile before I break your bloody arm!"

Ophelia opened her lips and raised them.

"No! No! No! You're showing me your fucking teeth! Give me a smile! I'm asking for *happy!* Can you not understand that?"

She smiled. "But I'm slipping," she said through her teeth.

"There. Good. Finally. Exactly like that. Keep smiling."

The camera clicked with the furious repetition of a machine gun, eight frames per second.

"I'm slipping," Ophelia said.

4

The morgue at Jackson Memorial in downtown Miami always reminded Trace of a vampire-filled nightmare he'd once had as a child. The vampires' eyes had glowed red as railway lamps from the open doors of a dark, windowless hallway, identical to the one Trace, Enrique, and Gary Nash took to Dr. Gonzales' office. This was a below-ground journey, sub-hospital. The morgue's smell ranged somewhere between bleach and vinegar with molded clothing—a smell strong enough to penetrate Trace's snotted-up nose.

Coroner Jesus Gonzales answered his office door after two knocks. His appearance varied little from other coroners: small-framed glasses, a head too big for its body, bald at the crown, circular specs, mad-scientist hunch to his posture, the white lab coat.

The *Igore* factor on Gonzales was especially high. He relished the tragically dead. Trace had heard him say so himself. Gonzales received epiphanies from opening corpses like moist books, sifting through their insides to discover what had gone wrong, what had caused this particular heart to quit its job.

Of course, Trace's own line of work brought him a similar understanding of what many wanted never to understand: Human beings were nothing more than self-propelled sacks of meat and blood and gelatinous bags, held together with tissue and bone. He'd seen bodies burned until they were crisp, shriveled skin strung over roasted skeleton. He'd once opened a closet door to find a severed, dripping head smiling down from a shelf. But these were hazards of the job, not rewards. What kind of freaks would devote their lives to such morbidity? Coroners would. Trace couldn't stand Gonzales. He couldn't stand any of them.

And judging from the iced-over glares Gary Nash kept firing Gonzales' way, it didn't seem the man cared too much for Gonzales either. Then again, it was likely the girl's father didn't care for much right now. The wealthy and renowned real estate mogul Gary Nash hadn't spoken anything save empty pleasantries since Trace and Enrique had picked him up at the airport and brought him here to the morgue.

Normal circumstances did not call for any such special treatment of a victim's parent, but this was not normal circumstances. Gary Nash was Rockefeller-rich. High profile. Captain Fulcher wanted Trace and Enrique's attention on the situation before the story became too interesting for too many people. National attention had a way of unhinging people.

Case in point: Gary Nash had already gone on TV in New York, swearing he would do whatever necessary to catch the person or persons who had sold or given his daughter drugs. The man was on a mission and, for this reason, Captain Fulcher wanted him chaperoned a while. A man so powerful and this anguished could destabilize a scenario quick. Even by making a televised vow to persecute, as if he alone were the law, Gary Nash had already taken a step towards making things far more complicated than necessary.

The special attention asked of Trace and Enrique meant their current investigation into the murder of a retired Argentine couple would have to wait. There was also the homicide of a homeless, hippie musician, but that hadn't been going anywhere anyway.

Gonzales took them down two more hallways, past a door marked "*Authorized Personnel Only / Solamente Personal*

Autorizado," and into darkness. He knuckled a light switch up and two sets of fluorescent paneling flickered strobe-like before remaining on. The room before them was lined with ceiling-high shelves housing manila folders, pregnant with paper. There were steel cabinets containing drawers containing God-knew-what. In the center of the room, illuminated starkly by the fluorescents, stood an examination table with a dead person on it, covered by a sheet.

Gary Nash walked to the table's side, clutching himself the whole way, like he'd been punched in the stomach, each step slower than the last. He worked his hands into his pockets and studied the shape beneath the sheet, in awe of it.

Gonzales came around to the bed's other side. "We need you to take a quick look."

Using two fingers, he lifted the sheet by the corner nearest Nash.

From where he stood, Trace could see only her left arm, pale and dormant at her side. The girl's father, staring down at her, blocked the rest.

"Sir?" Enrique called. In a black suit, skinny blue tie, and horn-rimmed shades, Enrique resembled an IRS agent. A Venezuelan Blues Brother. "Mr. Nash?"

"Call me just 'Nash.'"

Gonzales lowered the sheet back into place.

Nash reached down, raised the sheet again, and lay the corner aside. His voice cracked. "What was it again...that she overdosed on?"

"Methamphetamine." Enrique approached the table. "It was in her nasal passages and on her tongue and in her blood and organs."

"You may or may not have known this," Gonzales put in, "but your daughter had a prolapsed mitral valve. A heart murmur. Means the valves of her heart were small. Tiny. Any interruption in blood flow could've been fatal. This indicates to me that she suffered congestive heart failure, then asphyxiated as —"

Gonzales went to cover the girl up again, but Nash rushed a hand in the way. "Don't touch her!"

"Sorry, sorry. I'm sorry." Gonzales stepped back and pushed his glasses up on his nose.

A loud silence followed.

Trace saw Enrique look back at him, then across at Gonzales, then over at Nash. He looked down at the girl and said nothing. *Good boy*, Trace thought. *Shut up, Enrique. Don't mess with the man.*

Nash's face folded in on itself and his shoulders trembled. He sobbed soundlessly.

Seeing an opening, Trace walked to the table and stood next to him. The fluorescent lighting, bouncing off the white sheets, hugged the girl's form in a soft and luminous fur. The skin around her joints was browning, the cells there disintegrating. The saffron flush of her jaws and cheeks sagged from lack of muscle tension, a G-force face. Trace was surprised to see the Y-shaped autopsy scars were visible, obviously from when the father had re-lifted the sheet. Another scar, he knew, was behind her neck from where the face and scalp had been peeled back, allowing access to her skull.

"Excuse me, sir, but for the sake of formal identification," Trace said, "is this girl your daughter? Holly Elizabeth Nash? No need to speak. A nod is enough."

There was another silence filled by the low hum of the fluorescents. Gary Nash nodded. He placed the back of his hand to his daughter's cheek and kept nodding.

The horizon glowed with blood-red cloud shingles while royal-blue waves massaged the shore. The day's dying light silhouetted A-framed couples, the occasional jogger huffing by, the occasional derelict stumbling zigzag.

Trace removed his shades to better see Nash as he continued walking, though Trace and Enrique had stopped. Nash halted a few yards ahead, replanted his hands in his pockets, the wind ripping into his hair. He scanned the beach as though searching for someone and his sight settled on the distant, pinpoint flashing of cruise ships, yachts, fishing boats, ocean freighters.

Nash had a seat in the sand. He crossed his legs and joined his arms around his knees. "The Atlantic Ocean," he said flatly. "I just felt like seeing it. Thanks for bringing me out here. I'm sure you both have far more urgent things you could be doing."

Trace could hardly hear him over the wind. He stepped closer and bent down. He drilled a finger in the sand. "You know, when I first moved here, I was about nineteen, super young. But I remember when there used to be nothing on South Beach but hotels full of old Northerners who'd moved here to die. Just wanted to be warm while they waited."

"This town," Nash said, still staring off at the ocean. "I have no clue how you people could live here. It's too hot. No one speaks English. Drugs everywhere. Homosexuals everywhere. Homeless, crazy people. These fashion idiots..."

Trace slap-wiped his hands and duck-walked a few steps further, then sat in the sand beside him. He snuck a look back at Enrique who stood statue-still, meditating on the departing sun, the fading light of which darkened him by the second. A stiff wind insisted his tie lay over the back of his shoulder. Beyond him, stretched the pastel, neon mural of Ocean Drive hotels.

"The quality of light," Trace said. "It's ideal for photography, I've heard. That's why the fashion industry keeps coming here." Nash looked at him, and Trace felt himself blush. "The others you referred to are here because nowhere else wants them," he continued. "We're at the bottom of the country. No place left to go, I guess."

Nearby, a lifeguard unloaded his green, graffiti-coated station. He took out floatation devices and flags and placed them into the back of a white Bronco. Trace had caught Nash watching the lifeguard, so he watched him also.

"Weird, but when I left New York this morning, there were four inches of snow on the ground," Nash said, still watching the lifeguard.

"How's your wife holding up?" Trace asked him.

"Carol?" His hand made a tiny, dismissive gesture. "What can I say? She's completely out of her head. Our doctor prescribed her some medicine to calm her down. I can't— " He shook his head. "What am I going to tell her? I tell her our daughter died smoking crack, she won't understand it. Not in a million years. *I* don't even understand it."

A pair of dark-panted legs appeared behind them and Trace looked up to check their owner: Enrique. "It wasn't crack," he said, and swallowed hard.

"She blames me," Nash went on, his voice coming ragged. "She was against Holly leaving home. At least for very long and by herself. I let that Allison Taylor woman talk me into it, then I had to turn around and talk my wife into it. My wife hasn't said so, but I know she blames me for this. She'll blame me forever."

Trace went to contradict him, but kept his mouth shut. Let the poor guy eject what he had to.

Nash lowered his head. "I made such an effort to talk my wife into it because I wanted Holly gone. Not dead, not this. But, Jesus. What we went through with that girl. I thought it was best for everyone that she leave for a while. Give us a break from each other."

Enrique squatted and placed a cigarette between his lips. He cupped his hands around a lighter. He attempted over and over to light the cigarette, but the wind forbid it.

"She was a horror. A pain," Nash said. "God, from the day she was born. She was a breech baby." He made a sad laugh. "But, anyway, this was what she wanted. Be a ballerina, a famous supermodel, then singing and making records, then a big movie star, then...whatever else popped into her head. She was flunking out of school anyway. And she—Christ—and she *hated* us. *Hated.* How *dare* I give her everything she ever needed?"

"You did what you could, sir," Enrique said, as if he could

know such a thing. The cigarette remained unlit in his mouth.

There was nothing else said for a great while until Nash scratched his chin with his thumb. "Hm," he said. "I need a shave."

Trace couldn't help but notice Nash's watch. A simple, silver stretch band model. Silly, but from what he'd heard of the guy, Trace might've expected the watch to be gold with diamond studs, rubies encircling a sapphire face.

The lifeguard started up his Bronco and its headlights cut a path of light across them. The Bronco revved once, scooted forward, then turned around. The headlights jostled from the sand.

"Mr. Nash, autopsy puts your daughter's death at about 3:30 in the morning," Trace said, "a little before we have people seeing this Drexel character leave her room, the same guy who drew on her and left his name and phone number behind. According to what her roommate told us, he's the one who likely gave her drugs. I understand you want to prosecute him, but we have to warn you: This sort of thing is nearly impossible to convict in court."

Nash had no response to this.

"I suppose what I'm saying is," Trace added, "we'll bring the guy in. But there's absolutely no guarantee he'll see much jail time, if any."

Nash nodded, but the thoughts on his face were from elsewhere. A woman with a child holstered on her hip passed near. Nash watched her while he spoke. "Maybe this *was* my fault. I should've spent more time with her. I shouldn't have been down on her so much."

Enrique rested a hand on Nash's shoulder. "Don't upset yourself. Why don't you let us drive you back to your hotel? Get some rest."

"She was a baby, wasn't she?" Nash said to Trace. He turned his full face on him. "I didn't even realize she was eighteen already...*Eighteen*. In a year, when she's nineteen..."

Nash froze. He appeared to be waiting for a response to his

mistake. Trace didn't know what else to do but nod. When Nash unbent himself and stood, he joined him. Enrique stood as well.

"What about that woman and John Belushi?" Nash asked. "I've had my lawyer do some research for me."

"John Belushi?" Trace shook his head.

"You're talking about Cathy Smith?" Enrique asked Nash. "Yeah, Belushi's wife had her prosecuted for giving him the speedball that killed him. It was a long time ago, but you're right. It's not unheard of."

Trace scratched the back of his neck and winced from a stiffness there. "Like I told you, we'll do everything we can. If we get this guy for anything, it'll be for violating his parole. The worst might be second-degree manslaughter, for his neglecting to get help. Even then, he'll only be looking at nine months, maybe even less."

"No problem." The bewilderment had vanished from Nash's voice. "I'll hire a dog pound of attorneys if I have to. The most rabid I can find. Even if this guy can't be jailed, I'll make him wish he was."

Trace replied evenly, "Sir, you could hire *God* for your attorney, but unless this guy flat-out confesses he gave her drugs which he knew would kill her, it'll take a miracle to get any court to convict with evidence this circumstantial on a charge this vague," Trace paused, watching him. "But if your mind is set, whatever. We'll do what we can to help you. It's what we're here for."

"Give me five minutes alone with him and I'll find out exactly what happened last night, second by second. It won't be hard."

"It'd be best to leave enforcement to us, okay?"

"Detective Strickland..."

"Call me 'Trace.'"

"Trace, my daughter, my little girl, isn't alive anymore. If this piece of shit played a part in that fact, then I want his head and I will have his head. I realize there's no way I can possibly make you understand how I feel, but there it is. While you guys work to get him, *I* will work to get him. I'm not leaving Miami until I do."

"Ah, dammit, damn," Enrique mumbled. He was turning one direction, then another, but remained unsuccessful in keeping the wind away from his lighter.

Nash gave a slow, deliberate look between them before wandering off in the direction of the ocean. He stood lengthily at the surf's edge before removing his shoes and socks and rolling up his pant legs. He entered the water and struggled against the current until he was hip-deep. There, he stood and regarded the waves in the same uncomprehending way he had his daughter's body. His figure appeared diminished, overwhelmed by the ocean's immensity, a dot against all that blue.

A few yards from him, a pelican dive-bombed into the water, then resurfaced, afloat, the pouch part of its beak convulsing with its catch.

5

Drexel showed up at the bar clean-shaven but seemingly wearing the same clothes from last night. They appeared cut with creases, slept-in. While feeding from a box of *Chicken McNuggets*, Drexel marveled at the events of some party last night, relating to Trace how he'd even banged this girl in a closet.

Late afternoon, when Drexel next opened his eyes, he was in Ophelia's bed and she was gone. He rose onto his elbows to check the room for her, but remembered she was being photographed for a European wedding catalog that day.

During the whole story, Trace said little, only to remark "Wow" or "No way." Drexel didn't appear to notice his friend's discomfort and Trace didn't mind. He was good with only listening anyway. It was one of the biggest reasons they'd always gotten along so well.

Trace had found Drexel's phone number, then called him, inviting him for a drink to catch up, work his way into seeing what the story was, one old friend to another. Hopefully help the guy out if he could. However, five beers later and Drexel hadn't stopped talking, during which he kept popping something from a pill bottle, each pill chased with a swig of *Pepto Bismol*, which was next chased with more beer.

Seeing Drexel for the first time in nearly a decade, at this dive bar, surrounded by the kind of crinkled-paper people who would *have* drinks at a dive bar right before nightfall on New Year's Day, Trace didn't feel like he was sitting with Drexel, but an actor playing his role. A plagiarism. Suddenly the person from his memory had a body again.

Trace recalled the first time he'd ever seen him: Drexel was on stage, nude except for a G-string, rolling his hips, snake-like. His fingers were joined behind his neck while a grinning grandmother stuck dollar bills into his G-string's strap. Her younger companions spilled to their sides with laughter. This was back in Atlanta, in Tool's. Trace had come to apply for a job.

Trace's ambition for college quarterback stardom had been nullified in the game, Savannah High vs. Augusta, in which a four hundred-pound boy threw himself on Trace, forcing his left leg to fold backwards, driving his femur bone through the skin of his thigh. The bones and tendons healed, but doctors warned that another similar injury would likely result in amputation. Trace loved football, though not as much as he loved owning two legs.

Plan B was to try and make a lot of money somehow since this was generally considered a smart thing to try and do. Problem was, there wasn't a college founded that would accept him with his grades, not without a scholarship. Due to an all-encompassing lack of interest, he'd barely passed high school. Might not have if Coach hadn't harassed the teachers so much.

Trace knew that by neglecting his studies, he'd fouled up in some fundamental way. But it couldn't have been helped. He'd only cared about football and girls. School was six hours of sitting there. There was some pressure from his father to become a policeman like himself, but Trace wasn't ready for that. He was too cool for anything so predictable.

His life eventually found its course thanks to television, the favorite anesthesia of the unemployed and undecided. It was a tabloid news show spotlighting *The Chippendale Dancers.* In exchange for money and travel all that seemed required of them was to dance and creatively take their pants off. Didn't feel like a bad way to make a living, at least temporarily. The story had aired because of an audition being held in Atlanta, a two hundred and fifty-mile drive from Savannah, Trace's home.

Trace's audition went disastrously. It hadn't occurred to him *The Chippendale's* committee would expect him to perform his own dance routine, bring his own music. He figured the sole requirement was to be somewhat handsome, not a professional *dancer*. Borrowing a tape from another candidate, he improvised. But after a few seconds, the head of the committee thanked him and asked him, please, to stop.

Already enthused by the idea of moving to Atlanta, getting out on his own, Trace checked the classified section of *The Atlanta Constitution*. There, he saw an ad for a strip club seeking "Male Dancers. Apply in person." He prepared a routine this time, but it was never asked for. He was told by a man and his wife to take his clothes off, turn around. He worried the surgery scar on his thigh might be a problem, but the married couple (the owners, Bob and Lydia Toole) hired him on the spot. Trace moved into an apartment less than a mile away.

He and Drexel bonded fast. It was a friendship spawned by a similarity in age, an overwhelming need for stimulation, and the desperate pursuit for it. The more turbulent the stimulation, the better.

As male strippers, finding sex was as easy as ordering takeout. Female customers slept with them as if it were not a choice, as if Trace and Drexel were deified by the stage lights, the squeals of embarrassed pleasure. Who could blame a girl if she wanted to have fun, only for one night? No strings, only a well-built boy who looked like he'd pirouetted off the cover of some romance novel?

As far as the two friends were concerned, sex was the best drug in the world. But not that this didn't keep them from getting off chemically as well. Trace preferred smoking pot to anything heavier, but Drexel developed a fondness for dropping acid before his shift. He was even once suspended from the club for three months after having crawled about the stage on all fours, growling like a dog, doing so even when it was time for the next dancer, Trace, who had to perform around him.

There was also speed, Special K, hash. All Trace knew was that he wanted to live forever and, at the age of nineteen, saw no indication this wasn't plausible.

Then, during an otherwise normal Tuesday, came The Night of The Modeling Scout. She worked for Men of K-Oz, a male modeling agency on Miami Beach. She attended Toole's for a bachelorette party, approaching Drexel within minutes. She wanted to send him to South Beach, take some test shots, see how they came out.

Two months later, Drexel was on the cover of *British GQ*.

Trace tried, in vain, not be jealous of Drexel's success. It was confounding. What was it about this guy? Drexel never worried about anything yet always came out ahead for it. Were Trace himself to operate with the same recklessness, he owned little doubt he'd be dead or disabled.

Trace gave in, followed his father's path by joining the police department. He'd already gotten accustomed to dressing like a cop as part of his strip act anyway. He chose the force in Miami Beach to remain with his best friend, but more importantly because MBPD didn't care about his past. If stripping once got the bills paid, fine, so long as his record was clean.

He and Drexel stayed in touch for a few months until that faded. The next Trace heard about Drexel was that he'd spent five months in jail for statutory rape. Trace kept his distance afterwards. In fact, once he became a homicide detective, he kept as much length as possible between Homicide Detective Trace Strickland and Professional Male Dancer Trace Strickland. The day was coming when his colleagues would find out, but he prayed it wouldn't be over this. Or over anything else for the rest of his life.

Now, sitting in this South Beach bar with Drexel, Trace felt no different than if he were sitting with an ex-girlfriend, up against the wall that distance and time had built between them. He couldn't help it. It gave him the creeps.

◆ ◆ ◆

Drexel scratched his eyebrow. "Mmmmm, I've got a pimple in my eyebrow," he said. He twitched, jerking his chin in, itchy brow pressed over his eye. "Hey, did I introduce you to my two friends over here?"

Without turning, Drexel pointed a thumb over his shoulder at two girls in a booth, both holding a manufactured beauty, of having been inflated from boxes. One owned blond hair clumped like strands of yarn. She wore a terry cloth crop top and cotton hot pants. The other girl wore a tight, zebra-striped dress. She had red hair cut into a high fade.

"Rachelle and Connie," Trace said. "You introduced us two seconds ago."

"The one with red hair? Rachelle? You know she's Allison Taylor's daughter, right? Rachelle's the one I told you about. I chowed on her box while her girlfriend watched me. Man!" Drexel placed his hand on the bar and pushed away from it. He balanced his stool on its back legs.

It was pause enough, so Trace went for it: "Drex, there's something I need to talk to you about."

"That other girl over there, Connie, the blond, she has the face of an angel, doesn't she? Can't you picture her with a pair of white, fluffy wings?"

"I know you were with Holly Nash before she died last night."

"Who?"

"It's why I've called you here. I wanted to talk to you as a friend rather than a cop first."

"Am I in trouble?"

"*You* tell me."

The bartender—a tight T-shirted, pro-wrestler candidate —swiped away their ashtray. He slapped it against the inside of a trashcan and slid it back. The empty ashtray wobbled like a coin, faster and faster until it stopped.

"I already told you," Drexel said. "I don't remember."

"A powerful man's daughter is dead from an overdose and she had your name and hotel number written on her arm. And you were seen leaving her room, running. You actually could be in some peril here, man."

Drexel shook his head. "She did mention her dad was a big deal."

"Thought you didn't remember anything."

"I do now. It's coming back. Yeah, I remember the whole thing."

"What happened?"

"She started passing out, and I went to get help, but then I passed out too and guess I forgot. I sort of remembered this morning, but then I convinced myself she was okay because I needed her to be."

"She's not okay."

"That drug was laced! Had to be." Drexel took a long pull from his beer and lit another cigarette. He let go several blue breath clouds. "Don't guess that would exactly help me though, would it? What am I going to do? It was an accident."

Trace lit a cigarette of his own, his first in years. "Turn yourself in and get a lawyer."

Drexel nodded while sipping. The bottle's mouth bobbed with his lips. He set the beer back down. "I'm sure you're right. You're the law now. You must be right."

"I'll do everything I can to help you."

"Would you? That'd be swell."

His attention became stolen by the two girls behind them, Rachelle and Connie. Trace had noticed them looking at Drexel, then looking at each other, then laughing into their hands. As they'd done twice before, they called Drexel's name and engaged him in shouted banter, the subject of which mainly concerned people the three of them knew. Like that, that easy, Drexel was distracted and jovial again. It was astonishing. A young girl was dead.

As he did the other times, Trace still felt relieved to be

sidelined. He did things— scooted the ashtray closer between them, lit another cigarette, worked at removing the label from his bottle—only for the sake of movement, the illusion of pre-occupation. He felt sad.

Once Drexel's conversation with the girls had dribbled empty, he turned to Trace, leaned over. "My dude, magical things are brewing. Two of them, two of us. You up for it?"

"Up for what?"

"If I'm going to prison I might as well have fun on my last night as a free man, right?"

"That won't necessarily happen. Prison, I mean."

"Won't necessarily *not* happen either. Let's do it. Like old times."

"Drexel, you do understand that the girl you had sex with last night is dead and people are blaming you for it."

"Yeah, my life is over. Give me this one last joy though? It'll probably be the last one I ever have. Cool? Come with us."

"You know I can't. That'd be insane."

Drexel slapped his hand on the bar and sang-said: *"Don't leave me now!"* He stood from his stool and reared his arm as if to fastball his beer bottle at the opposing mirror. But his arm shot too far back, and he fell backwards to the floor.

"Fucking—" He looked around himself, dismayed, laughing. "And he's down!"

Trace reached to help him up, but when he got hold of his elbow, Drexel grabbed Trace's shirt and worked at pulling him down too, laughing harder. They were locked this way with Trace hissing at him to get the hell up when the two girls came over. They got Drexel on either side beneath his arms and helped lift him. After he was on his feet, he laid his arms around the girls' shoulders and hung his head.

Trace noticed the bartender watching them with both hands on the bar, on the verge of turning scornful.

"I'm getting him a cab, right now," Trace let him know.

He followed the two girls as they walked Drexel out of the bar. Once on the sidewalk, Drexel raised his head, resurrected.

"Where we going? Let's go somewhere. Rachelle, where you staying?"

"I'm still living with Mom, but our house is huge," Rachelle said. "Mom's usually zonked on her pills by now anyway. You guys want to come over?"

Trace stepped to the curb and searched the passing traffic for a taxi. Trace decided he would do the sensible thing and go home. He would get some rest and hope Drexel turned himself in the next morning. Make things easy.

When a taxi pulled to the curb, Trace stood aside while the other three got in back. After a minute, Drexel poked his head out the window.

"*Hellooooo*," he said. "Earth to Trace. You coming with us or what?"

"Sure, I'll sit up front," Trace said. And he did, nearly slamming his foot in the door.

6

The courtyard of Gary Nash's hotel remained populated by small pockets of partiers, even at three in the morning. He stood watching them from his fifth-floor balcony. It was a beachfront luxury hotel with a nautical-sounding name and thirty-three floors. Nash choose the fifth floor, the lowest available. He wanted to keep grounded. More in touch. The sounds of the party had drifted in and out of his room since early the previous evening. He hadn't slept a wink, but not from the noise. Not the noise outside his head anyway.

He turned his attention to the gun in his hand, a .32 caliber he'd purchased from the hotel bellman's cousin's brother-in-law's father. Something like that.

Nash's relationship with firearms had started in earnest at age fourteen when his parents sent him to New York Military Academy. He'd earned top academic honors two years in a row before receiving a Finance Degree at Columbia. After graduating, he joined his father's real estate development company. Within five years, "the son" single-handedly changed Nash Properties into the largest of its kind in the Northeast, thanks mainly to New York's tax concessions for city-improvement projects.

Nash placed the barrel of the gun into his mouth and closed his lips around it. He used his thumb to pull the trigger.

Click.

The gun salesman had possessed every manner of lethal merchandise imaginable, except, that is, for bullets. A safety policy. Nash would get bullets later. After a nap maybe. He lowered the gun, raised his cellphone. He dialed home. Five rings. Voicemail. He dialed his wife's number. Same thing. He left a message this time:

"Checking in," he said. "I've been trying to call you, Carol, but no one answers. I'm going to stay in Miami a bit longer and take care of some things. Might be a little while before I see you. Keep it together, okay? Any reporters call, hang the hell up. Tell your friends to come visit if they need you. Until then, don't worry about anything. I'll be back no later than tomorrow, I swear." He paused. "I love you much."

He hung up, thought his voice message over, and re-dialed his wife. "Me again. Wanted you to know I saw her and she's still beautiful. She always will be, Carol. Maybe you'll feel better once you see her. Which reminds me: Don't worry about the funeral. Don't worry about anything. I will take care of it all. You know I will."

His voice wilted and he ended the call. Nash clenched his throat, held back from crying by shutting his eyes. He wiped his forehead with the back of his hand, the same hand holding the gun. He lowered the weapon and held it in both hands.

Nash was eleven when he'd fired his first gun. His father had taken him behind their summer house in The Catskills for a firing demonstration, said it was a rite of passage every man should do with his son sooner or later, if for no other reason than to learn the proper respect needed. Nash didn't remember the kind of gun it'd been, only it was a small-caliber handgun that actually went "pow!" if you spelled the sound.

His father had set up an array of cans and bottles as targets. Though Nash only managed to hit one can, his father shouted encouragement, clenching a stiff, meaty hand on Nash's shoulder. His father next gave him a speech which included warnings about guns not being toys and other such advice that would've been unclear only for a maniac.

Was this what he was now? All depended on his reasons for buying the gun, but he hadn't analyzed those yet. This was another on his list of things to do after a nap.

Down in the courtyard, he saw a young couple having a bad night. He couldn't hear them, but the swiftness of their gestures suggested an intense argument. The girl began walking away, but the boy grabbed her. He buried his face between her shoulder blades and held her tight. The girl continued walking, which tilted their embrace awkwardly. Nash aimed the gun at them, holding his arms straight out, elbows locked. He gripped the handle firm with both hands as his father had shown him.

Nash needed to get back to his wife, of course, but it was important he meet with Drexel Waters first. The gentleman had ended his daughter's life, so seemed only fair. Nash deserved a brief interview at least, didn't he? From the man who had helped bring her into this world to the man who had escorted her right out of it. Nash deserved an explanation of sorts.

"Pow," he whispered. "Pow pow."

7

As Trace knew they inevitably would be, he and Drexel were naked. Every game of "Truth or Dare" Trace had ever played ended without clothes. It always started out with everyone asking for "truths," then dissolved exclusively into "dares." Soon, no one even asked which was preferred.

Rachelle and Connie sat in their underwear on the side of a bed, wine glasses at their feet. Trace sat with Drexel, cross-legged on the floor. The four of them were in Rachelle's bedroom, bigger than Trace's apartment. Allison Taylor's mansion, located on Hibiscus Island in Biscayne Bay, was a flamingo-pink monstrosity having once belonged to Al Capone, the infamous prohibition mobster.

The four of them had had to tiptoe upstairs so as not to awaken Mother.

Rachelle's bedroom contained crayon-yellow walls and a bamboo furniture theme. Surrounding them were framed pictures of twig-limbed people with baskets on their heads. A lamp on the nightstand was the room's single light, puppeteering top-heavy shadows on the walls.

During the introductory truth portion of the game, Trace confessed he was sexually attracted to both Rachelle and Connie, to not having lost his virginity until he was seventeen, and to sometimes fantasizing about other women when he would make love with his fiancée.

Drexel, refusing to be serious, confessed to having a hermaphrodite as a mother/father, to wanting a tattoo of his own face at the tip of his penis, to having had sex with chickens.

Rachelle confessed that once, after a party in which she'd unknowingly smoked a joint laced with PCP, she awoke in her own bed with half her clothes missing and no idea how she'd gotten there. Connie confessed to having sexual fantasies which involved multiple cartoon characters, both male and female. At the age of twenty-six, they were both veteran fashion models approaching retirement already. Rachelle was thinking of becoming a makeup artist. Connie was down on Christmas Break from Boston U.

It was Trace's turn again. He did what was expected and dared one of the girls to finish undressing: Connie. He would have picked Rachelle, but he liked her more and didn't want her to know. He simply didn't understand himself sometimes.

"I got a better idea." Drexel poured himself the last of the wine. Through the blue tinting of the glass, the wine resembled motor oil. "Why don't you, Rachelle, take off Connie's underwear?"

"Hey, hey, hey," the girls clamored, more or less simultaneously. "It's not your turn. Be quiet!"

Trace pushed his lips together and vacuumed at the end of a joint. "Sounds like a good suggestion to me," he said, his voice strained from holding in the smoke. He passed the joint to Rachelle.

"You're such a bad influence, Drexel. You truly are." Rachelle accepted the joint, brought it to her lips, and re-lit it with a lighter. She closed her eyes and inhaled sharply.

Drexel took the joint next, the smoke turning orange from the orange light of the orange lampshade. "Yo!" he said. "It's your guys' turn. Get naked!"

The girls stopped giggling and looked at each other. Rachelle shrugged. She reached down and took hold of Connie's ankles and elevated her legs until they lay across her lap. The girls looked at each other again, snorted more laughter into their hands.

"Oh my God, I am going to lose it right now." Drexel butterflied his knees. "Take 'em off! Take 'em off!"

Tossing her hair back and sliding over, Rachelle hooked her fingers beneath the straps of Connie's panties and eased them downwards. Connie lifted her ass slightly to help the panties in passing over her hips. Rachelle got on her knees to finish pulling the panties free of Connie's feet. She returned to the edge of the bed and lay Connie's legs across her lap again. She stroked them with the front, then the back of her hand.

Connie laughed and jiggled her legs. She twisted her hips. "Tickles."

The stroking ascended slowly until halting mere centimeters from her pussy. Rachelle played her fingers through Connie's slight pubic hair, giving it a gentle pull. She traced her fingers further downwards until reaching the soft pink creases there. Rachelle rubbed the tip of her index finger down the length of Connie's pussy, pushing but not entering. Connie gasped and squeezed her legs together.

Rachelle abruptly folded her hands in her lap. "Okay, my turn to dare," she said.

Drexel fell backwards and wailed, grief-stricken.

Trace could feel the sweat in his chest hair.

"You girls are killing us!" Drexel cried.

"Okay. Now." Rachelle wagged a finger between them. "It's *my* turn to dare one of *you*."

"Hold on." Trace stood, almost before he realized he'd done so. His hands covered his privates. "I've got to get going."

Everyone looked at him confused, then Connie bellowed, "Oh yeah. *Now* you do!"

Trace scanned the floor for his clothes. He located his underwear and stepped into them.

Drexel sat up and unfolded his legs. "You're leaving?"

"You guys have fun. Don't let me stop you."

"What happened?" Rachelle asked Connie.

"No, I'll bet he's weirded out because of his fiancée," Drexel explained. To Trace: "I heard what happened to her, man. Super sorry to hear it."

Trace hurried into his jeans. "No, it's nothing. It's me. I've got—" He filled one shirt sleeve with his arm, then the other. "I can't be doing this. I don't know what the hell's wrong with me."

"You feel like what's happened to Cassie is your fault, don't you?"

Trace stared at him, stunned. "What?"

Drexel flinched. "Oops, was that rude? I don't know how to talk to you anymore. Ever since you became...a fucking cop and all."

"A *what*?" Connie asked. She hid her crotch with her hand, suddenly shy. "He doesn't have to stay if he's not comfortable."

Cheeks sizzling with embarrassment, Trace fastened the bottom two buttons of his shirt. He pocketed his socks and slid his bare feet into his shoes. He opened the door and was about to leave, hopefully before Drexel could get another word out. Drexel called his name.

Trace stopped at the door. "I've got to go. Sorry. This is crazy."

"You're not *enjoying* this?" Drexel asked him.

"I need some sleep. That's all. Late night."

"So you're splitting this very second?"

"And I have a cold."

"How will you get home?"

"Cab, I guess."

"You sure?"

"Yeah."

"Whatever, man. I'll call you, I guess." Drexel eyed him, giving his best hurt look. "Oh, and we'll get that situation figured out, the one we talked about." He held up his hand for Trace to slap-shake, which he did, crossing the room to do so. Their hands stayed together, squeezed. "I've missed you like a brother," Drexel said. "I was super psyched when you called me.

Even though it was for a sucky reason."

"Sure, great seeing you."

"We'll hang out again, right? We'll go surfing."

After they'd dropped hands, Trace stepped back and drank in the room and for an instant everything became remarkably vivid: the floor, the bed, his hand, the bikini lines in twin white arcs through the brown of Connie's thighs, Rachelle's puzzled, watching face, the glazed picture of the hula girl strumming a ukulele under the palm tree on the ashtray on the floor.

"Yeah, we'll get together," he said. He made a gun of his thumb and forefinger, pointed it at Drexel, and shot him. "We'll have fun again."

"*This* isn't fun?"

"You know what I mean." But Trace himself wasn't even sure what he meant. He apologized. He said bye to everyone. He apologized again. He left the room and he closed the door behind him.

8

The next morning, Trace sat in a plush couch while enjoying a screwdriver. This was on the patio portion of a hotel lobby, facing Ocean Drive. A tight parade of tourists sauntered by, every one of them with a baseball cap and sunglasses, shielding themselves from the mid-day South Florida glare.

Trace had already called Drexel at nine o'clock, told him he would come give him a lift to the police station. Get it over with. Drexel agreed, said give him till noon, till he could get back to his hotel. And here Trace sat outside the agreed-upon hotel and no Drexel. No answer from his cellphone either, not even by one-thirty.

Meanwhile Enrique had called twice. Trace assured him that his friend would show up. Drexel wasn't this crazy. Give him more time.

Trace finished his screwdriver, pushed himself to his feet. He entered the lobby. The desk clerk was a heavy-set woman, boulder-breasted, brass-shaded hair stretched back into a needle-straight ponytail. As she was asking Trace if she could help him, a ruler-thin, curly-haired girl entered his periphery.

"Any sign of him yet?" he asked the desk clerk. "You remember what he looks like, right?"

"He's been a guest here for a few months, sir."

"Got it. Just very important, okay?"

"Hi, Janine," the girl said to the desk clerk, a slight accent. Southern maybe. "Have you seen Drexel?"

"Who are you?" Trace asked her.

Ophelia turned to him and that's when Trace got his first full—*eyes the color of shallow surf, lashes thick as thorns, arrow-point eyebrows, puffy lips, sandy-blond hair coiling and uncoiling into hectic curls around her shoulders, bangs braided with beaded ends, Daisy Duke shorts, legs smooth and shiny as varnished wood, rainbow tie-dye T-shirt knotted across the midriff, nut-brown torso lassoed by a butterfly belly chain*—look at her.

She returned his stare. "Who are *you?*"

"Detective Trace Strickland. Drexel isn't here yet."

"Does he know detectives are looking for him?" she asked, not missing a beat.

"I was supposed to meet him here almost two hours ago."

"I don't know where he is. Swear to God."

"Easy, easy. I'm an old buddy of his. I'm here to help him."

"Yeah? I'm here to wring his neck and stomp on his face."

"Maybe we can wait together then. Buy you a drink?"

"No thank you."

"I'd like to ask you some questions though. Besides, I'm a police detective and I can tell you all about it. I'm fascinating."

Ophelia crossed her arms. "Do I have a choice?"

"It won't take long."

"Let's at least go somewhere private? I work with a lot of these people."

Trace made a quick bow, which was a rare gesture for him. He couldn't recall bowing for too many people before. Maybe never. The flirty easiness of her was intoxicating. "Lead the way," he said.

He sat beside her on the balcony, two stories up, both of them with their legs hanging over the side, beneath the railing.

The hotel's courtyard spread out before them, divided in two, the closest half being concrete. It contained a spread-out array of stone benches and tables, potted flesh-colored tongue plants, blood plants, gator plants, plus gaunt, drowsy palm trees with large, feathery leaves. The courtyard's further half was sand with wooden lounge chairs lining both sides of a bamboo fence.

"How long have you been going out with him?" Trace asked her.

"Couple years."

"Any idea where he's disappeared to?"

"Doesn't answer *my* calls either."

"Why are you so angry with him?"

"He doesn't answer my calls." She lit a cigarette while holding it in the corner of her mouth. She looked at him. "What has Drexel done? Do I get to know?"

Trace lit his own from hers. He gagged, not ready for it. He coughed hard. When he was finally able to stop, he brought his hands around his throat. "Boy."

"You okay?" she asked.

"Recently started smoking again." He wheezed and his eyes teared. He wiped at the tears with the back of his hand. "What's your name, by the way?"

"Ophelia. You're his good friend and he's never mentioned me to you?"

He looked at her. "'Ophelia?' Like from Shakespeare?"

"Like from a trailer park in North Florida. What did Drexel do? Is he in big trouble?"

"You'll have to talk to *him* about that."

"Did you check inside his room? Maybe he's hiding."

"I knocked and no one answered."

"You couldn't get a key? You're the police."

"Not legal for me to enter a hotel room without the guest's permission, not if they're not there. Not without a warrant. *You* don't happen to have a key, do you?"

"Never gave me one."

"You're his girlfriend. Why aren't you both staying together at the same hotel?"

"He made me get my own hotel room, so he could have his private space." Ophelia crossed her arms over the bottom rail and lay her head there. "I need a new boyfriend."

"I'm tempted to volunteer." He kept his eyes on his hands while they fussed over each other. "I'm not the kind of guy who says this sort of thing to someone I just met, but I have to tell you that when I saw you back there, from first sight I was—" He pressed a hand to his chest. "I was floored."

She blinked at him, not understanding. She mouthed the last few words of what he'd said.

"What I'm saying is..." He rolled his hand to stir up the right phrases. "You're mega-ultra-beautiful. You're perfect."

She pointed a finger at herself. "Perfect? Not even close."

"You're my old friend's girlfriend and I almost don't even care. I can't stop myself."

"You drunk?"

Trace shook his head, steadied it with his hand on top. "A touch. Buzzed. And you're way too involved in the case. Anyway, I'm sure Drexel is crazy about you. You must be very happy."

"I must be." She rubbed her foot. "Ah, my foot's asleep." She brought her legs out from beneath the railing and folded her knees near her chest. She tucked her bottom lip behind her front teeth and micro-examined her toes. "Look, don't be offended, but you're not my type anyway."

Trace gave a minuscule shrug. "I grow on people." He gazed across the courtyard, at the wind molesting its plant life. The sky was blank, giving back nothing but the urine-tinted glow of the sun, muffled by a single, gray cloud sheet. Atop the hotel, three stories above, a sun-bleached American flag rippled lazily in the wind.

She furrowed her brow. "Can you at least tell me if he's going to jail?"

"It's becoming a possibility. Avoiding me sure isn't helping."

A wall of wind pushed its way between them. Trace stood. He cocked his cigarette butt between his thumb and middle finger. "Ready? Shooting star. Make a wish." He flicked the finger, launching the cigarette, the glowing orange dot ascending, descending, breaking apart against the concrete ground.

"I did," she said. She looked up at him. "I made a wish. Did you?"

"It never works. Here's my card," he told her. "Please, let me know if you hear from him."

9

There was Gary Nash, supposedly having pulled in eight hundred mil last year, now surrounded by the plush décor of a luxury hotel room; but with an unshaven face, hair askew, clothing slashed full of creases, he now more closely resembled a homeless wino rather than owner of one of the nation's most prolific real estate companies. He'd almost grown a beard, and he smelled. He sat slumped within a C-shaped sofa, his arms across its top. His head was tilted back with a wet washcloth covering his forehead.

Seeing him from across the room, Trace could remember sitting in the same position, in his own apartment, not more than four months ago. For reasons not too much unlike Nash's. The grief could grind in like that, like a force, physically caving you.

Trace admired Nash. The man emitted such resilience. Even this current, crashed posture of his projected the image of a man anguished and shaken, but already recovering because he needed to. Trace found it difficult to meet the man's eyes though. Too much going on in there.

Before they were able to deliver their news, Nash had some of his own. He gave it to them after Trace and Enrique had had a seat in opposite, identically-designed sofas. The news: Mrs. Nash, his wife, was in the hospital as the result of an overdose. She'd taken too many pain pills. Whether by accident or on purpose, no one knew yet. She was in a coma. Nash was flying to La Guardia that night but would return to Miami by tomorrow evening.

The air stiffened, briefly muffling the possibility for speech. In his discomfort, Trace over-familiarized himself with the hotel room, carpeted in tan short-hair, the curtains and furniture covered with matching obtuse prints of midnight-violet and firehouse-red. Three walls were floor-to-ceiling glass, the front wall sliding open onto a room-sized balcony. Asiatic lily-filled vases sat about, the leaves and petals fanned like frozen explosions.

Nash raised his head and the washcloth rolled to his lap. "You were going to tell me something? My mother overdose on drugs now, too?"

"No, nothing so tragic," Enrique said. "But it's not the greatest news. Our man Drexel Waters was going to turn himself in, but apparently he's had a change of heart. He's disappeared."

"Think he's leaving the country?" Nash asked, then louder, sitting forward: "We have to stop him!"

Trace chuckled for some reason. "We'll find him. Don't worry. He'll be arrested."

"I thought that was the plan. Let's do it already."

"Look, Mr. Nash," Trace said, "if you want to see this guy serve a substantial amount of jail time, we're going to need more of a case for having him in there. We can prove he was in the room; we *can't* prove he did anything wrong."

This brought Nash to his feet. "You've got fingerprints and witnesses and an autopsy! God! What the hell else would any court need?"

"Problem is—" Enrique let a few beats pass, "Sir, we weren't there, but it's safe to assume your daughter took those drugs voluntarily. No one put a gun to her head. Nailing this guy for homicide is going to require much heavier evidence than anything we have now, which is not much."

Trace would've expected Nash to bristle at the suggestion that any blame should be placed on his daughter. To Trace's inexplicable disappointment, Nash simply began pacing. He massaged his left hand, then his right. From a kitchen counter, he lifted a glass of clear liquid in which the ice didn't float.

"Sir, we do have an idea," Enrique said. He gave Trace an anxious look. They'd debated long and hard over whether to present Nash with this idea, arriving at a "play-it-by-ear" conclusion, though only because Enrique persisted. Trace hated the plan but wasn't sure about how to go about opposing it yet. The whole situation was in danger of shining further light on what he wished would stay hidden.

Nash stopped with his hand over his mouth. He massaged his whiskered face. "An idea," he said. "I'm listening."

"Drexel Waters has a girlfriend named Ophelia," Enrique explained. "We're thinking, for the right amount of money, she could get him to talk about what exactly happened that night. We could pay her to hide a recording device on herself. Could help your case a lot."

Nash's laugh was mirthless. "You want to hire his girlfriend as an informant? This is my best hope? The girl strike you as the sort of person who'd rat on her boyfriend for money?"

"Not for the kind of money *we* could come up with. But the kind of money *you* might offer..."

Nash stared laser beams at the carpet and said nothing for a while, then asked, "Is that legal?"

Trace cleared his throat. "Mostly."

"Either it's against the law or it isn't. Don't spit something like that out at me without letting me know precisely what I'd be getting myself into."

"Getting this girl to record him isn't illegal, as long as we find a court order. Paying her to do it? Makes the legality complicated. That's all. Needs to be our secret."

"My being wealthy...Automatically means I'm corrupt, huh?"

"No, sir, not corrupt. Not in the least. Just...at an advantage."

"Detective Strickland..."

"Trace."

"When I went off to college, my father didn't give me a dime. He wanted to make sure I learned to appreciate what he'd made for us. And his dad before him. There were nights in my boarding room when I would eat a cheese sandwich and *Pop-Tart* as my single meal of the day because I couldn't afford anything else! I worked my ass off and suffered greatly for what I have. Get this straight: My success had *nothing* to do with cheating or doing things illegally. *Ever.*"

"Didn't mean to offend you." Trace opened his hands. "We're presenting you with an option. You said you would do anything. I wasn't nuts about the idea, either."

"Oh, but I didn't say I wouldn't do it," said Nash, a grin spilling across his face. "If it's my best option, then I'd like to explore it. Talk to his girlfriend and get back to me tomorrow night, after I fly back. Offer her, say, two hundred and fifty grand? Unless I'm under arrest now. Am I?"

"What about your little rags-to-riches speech?" Trace asked him. "I was pretty moved."

"I needed you to know what I'm about. Where I'm coming from. What I stand to lose if this all gets messed up. Now what if his girlfriend says no? Not even for a *million* dollars?"

Enrique scooted forward and stood. "Then that's that and we move on to something else. It's worth a try though. We did a solid background check and, trust me, this much money could be the best thing to ever happen for her right now."

Nash downed the last of his drink, walked back around, and fell into the sofa. "Of course, yeah, money's always the best thing that could ever happen for you." He set his glass on the floor and laced his fingers together. "Hell, look at what all it's done for me," he said, sadly addressing his folded hands.

10

Ophelia used her key to open the door to Drexel's hotel room. She stepped in. The lights were off, but she could still make out a shape on the bed.

"Drexel?" she called.

"Ophelia."

"What are you doing?"

"Lying here."

"Doing what?"

"Lying here."

"You are in a ton of trouble. What happened?"

She turned on the light. The hotel room wasn't a lot different from her own, except his was slightly bigger. It held cream-colored walls holding black & white photographs of air-brushed ocean life, mostly killer whales and dolphins. There was a tooth-white GE refrigerator with an ad sticker stuck diagonally across its door: MILK IS GOOD. An aqua-marine Dream Maker long surfboard stood propped against the far wall, crusty with wax.

Drexel lay on his bed with his arms at his sides. His left hand held a *Pepto Bismol* bottle, his legs crossed at the ankles. Contrasted with the warm blue and autumn-orange of his room, Drexel, all pale skin and dark clothing, resembled a displaced black & white movie character in a colorized film. Her Kermit the Frog doll lay on the pillow beside him, propped there haphazardly. Kermit's neck was arched, his mouth open, as though howling in agony.

She turned the light back off. "Your friend was looking for you. He's a detective."

"I'm aware of that, my love."

"What did you do? He wouldn't tell me."

"Some girl overdosed and died at the party the other night. The police are talking to everybody. No big deal."

"Why did you ghost him then?"

"Because I don't know anything about that girl."

"So tell him. You blew him off?"

Drexel drank deep from the *Pepto Bismol.* He twisted to his right, set the bottle on the floor, lay back again. "I will. Didn't feel like dealing with it now."

"Are you telling me the truth?"

"Of course, yes. Geez, you're worse than any cop, huh?"

"I deserve to know."

"Where did you disappear to that night anyway? You got another guy?"

"You care?"

Ophelia recalled that she was furious with Drexel but decided to let it go for now. She'd poisoned him, nearly killing him for all she knew. Anyway, she was too relieved for today to have been the last day of shooting with that mean British photographer, too relieved to finally be in the presence of someone who, in whatever dysfunctional way, loved and cared for her.

She dropped her purse atop a small pile of folded blankets, a random resting sight among dozens of other piles of stuff she kept meaning to put away for him. After unsheathing her feet from cork-bottom sandals, she sat, unbuckled her jeans, kicked her way out of them. She discarded her shirt wherever. She straddled his waist, facing him. Her hands pinned his shoulders. "Why won't you stop being bad?"

"You wouldn't have me any other way."

She lifted Kermit by the leg and discarded him, somersaulting, against the closet door. She raised her face above his. Her hair made a curtain around his head. "Why were you lying alone in the dark?"

Drexel cleared his throat. "Just thinking."

She shifted and lay her cheek on his forehead. She let her eyes wander to the blue, gauzy curtains, to the night-stand where several different mechanisms of communication and light competed for surface space. Her eyes drifted to where the wall folded and became the floor, to the shiny, flat thing in Drexel's right hand. Flat, *sharp* thing. She bent her head up for a better look.

"What is this?" She reached for it. "Is this that knife?"

He moved his hand off the bed. "Uh-uh."

She sat up. She made as if to bend in the hand's direction but retracted onto her knees. "Drexel! What is it then?"

He rolled his eyes, his head. "It was in my back pocket, okay? It was hurting my ass, so I took it out and started, you know, it was there in my hand. I forgot about it. Don't cause a drama over it. Not now. Please? I'm depressed enough."

"And you're lying here, just thinking, but with a knife?" She opened her hand at him. "Ain't cool. Give me it."

"'Cause why?"

"I'm fed up with you. I'm going to cut your heart out and feed it to you."

He lay the knife in her palm and her fingers closed around its handle. For a second, he didn't let go. He surrendered posses-sion by dropping his hand.

"You haven't been throwing it into the wall again, have you?" she asked him.

"Of course I have. Helps me think. And I'm getting pretty good at it, too. The handle didn't hit the wall but once today."

"Where'd you get this thing anyway? It's a sword."

"Bowie knife. It's one of the few things Daddy ever gave me."

She narrowed her eyes at him, puckered her lips. "Oh, yes, you poor, poor wounded child."

"Give it a toss," he told her. "Relieves stress. Make sure you throw it hard as hell or it won't stick in."

"I am not throwing a knife at the wall. Shut up."

"You want to. I know you do. People think you're so sweet and innocent, but deep down? Like, *real* deep down? You're demonic."

Ophelia turned the knife in the light. She lay the knife against his throat. "Can I cut your head off?" she asked him.

He moved the knife away with a slow, distracted hand sweep. "Don't do that."

"What happened to the meth I gave you?"

"It was laced with something. Bad. I threw it away. You should change where you're getting it from."

"Drexel holy shit oh my lord!" Ophelia placed a hand over her mouth. A wet, red triangle was growing into a polygon right below his Adam's apple. "Your neck!"

He froze. "What about it?"

"When you moved my hand, you—The knife...Your neck is bleeding!"

"My neck?" He felt errantly along the far side of his neck.

She drew her breath in with a hiss. "Ah, God. You're getting it on the pillow! It's coming out everywhere!"

"Everywhere?" He touched his neck again, looked at his fingers. "The fuck?"

Drexel made a move towards the bathroom, but she grabbed him.

"Let's do it," she said. "Like this. Right now. Covered in your blood. Fuck me."

He tried prying himself free of her, but she held on until he understood she was serious. He stopped moving. "You cut me on purpose, didn't you?"

She took his hand and guided it between her legs. She gently rubbed herself over his hand until his fingers found their way inside. Ophelia gasped. She grinded his hand.

"Get ready," she said, kissing his face. She grazed her pussy atop his fingertips, back and forth, harder. "I'm going to cut your heart out and feed it to you."

Digging, grabbing, clenching, looking, but not looking at a brass-framed picture on the nightstand, a photograph of herself as a wire-smiled teenager with shaggy, dog-eared ponytails, a paprika sprinkle of acne. Drexel had placed it on the nightstand as a joke, his warped way of being cute.

From the corner of her eye, she watched him watching her face. She winced from what he was doing, but it felt good. Very, very good.

"Feel it?" His voice came as an exhilarated whisper. "That's me in there...It's me...It's me...You feel me?"

She gripped his wrists and helped him go harder. She quickened her hips to meet his hand, which gripped the knife that was fucking her. He held his thumb over the blade, but she imagined it was cutting her anyway, that the knife was ripping her apart, bright euphoric sparks sprouting behind her eye sockets.

Ophelia sat at the end of the bed. Drexel slept, no problem, beneath the covers behind her. He snored, she thought, almost wrathfully.

She scratched her head and felt her hair move as one piece. The blood had clumped it together. She looked down at herself and, though it was dark, she could see she was covered in Drexel's blood, more so than she first thought. She needed a shower soon, a long one. Soon, but now. Maybe it was the absence of light to reveal things as they truly were, or maybe she was that tired, but it didn't bother her much. It was nature and nature was beautiful. Except what would housekeeping think when they saw the sheets? She would have to throw the sheets away and offer to pay for another set maybe.

Ophelia bent over and shuffled through the debris at her

feet. There had to be one somewhere; she'd bought so many. With the aid of the striped, gray moonlight slicing through the window blinds, she found a copy of what she'd been looking for, its corner visible from beneath the bed. She pulled the magazine out and opened it across her lap. Having looked at the picture at least once a week for the past few months, always whenever she felt melancholic, she knew the exact page number.

Page 83: a picture of Ophelia leaning over a bathroom sink before a mirror, applying acotine cream to her forearm, smiling as if no more blissful sensation existed.

Ophelia touched her magazine picture's navel, indicating to no one but herself, that this skinny bitch, the one rubbing lethal skin cream under her eyes, her expression unhappy, but not suicidal, looking a little hopeful at the same time, was her. Ophelia. This. A printed photograph seen around the world. Looking at the photo used to cheer her up, but it was this same photo which also gave her nightmares. In them, she was a photograph. Thin and papery. Caught in a pose forever.

Ophelia closed the magazine and let it slide to the floor. She saw the TV remote there. She picked up the remote, aimed, and pressed. The screen bloomed into a commercial for a mud bogging drag race at Marlins Park. The commercial depicted various dragster trucks exploding, flipping, and rolling, as if the attraction of the event were not the race itself, but the thrill of seeing people suffer through incredibly violent accidents.

No question Drexel was lying. It was the tainted meth which had killed that girl. What else could be bothering him so much? He acted too weird. Lying alone in the dark, "just thinking?" Throwing a knife into the wall? Avoiding a friend who happened to be a cop? It all pointed to the worst scenario thinkable.

The paranoia and panic pulsed throughout her nerves and her hands shook. She tried to remain calm by reminding herself that she knew someone now who could help her. A man of the law. He would know what to do. There had to be a way out of this. She didn't mean to kill anyone. Did she? Was this what she'd wanted? Who was she anymore?

Drexel sat up and threw something, startling her. Ophelia yelped.

There was a zing, then a thud against the wall.

The knife.

11

Trace and Enrique sat in the 4Runner outside Nash's bank, the bottom floor of a downtown high-rise. They sat parked near the front of the bank on Biscayne Boulevard, the sidewalks choked from hordes of morose people in business suits on their way to do business jobs. Meanwhile, the sun blazed brighter than ever, intense as the gaze of God.

Nash approached the passenger side and handed a suitcase to Enrique through his open window. Nash walked away down the sidewalk without another word.

Trace used his rearview while Enrique peered over his shoulder. The two detectives watched Nash, both of them perplexed by his decision to walk away rather than rejoin them in the car. Once Nash had disappeared among the walking dead, Enrique lay the case on his lap. He relaxed his neck, shut his eyes, lips moving as though in prayer. When he opened his eyes, he opened the suitcase. He slammed it closed. "Should we count it?"

Trace stared straight ahead. "Not here."

"At my bank then. I have a safety deposit box. I'll even put your name on it and give you a key."

"Fine. Then we're going surfing."

"The waves aren't exactly calling to me right now."

"Listen harder. We need to digest this, what we're doing.

Or *I* do anyway."

"Fine. Give me a lift though?"

They went surfing together at least once a week. Trace was the one who first invited Enrique to go, way back when they were rookies. Enrique had never surfed before, and failed so miserably at it, he became obsessed. He was like that. Trace himself was a decent surfer, though nothing contest-worthy. He didn't care. It was all about freedom, gliding above the ocean's push, the way the present condensed itself into a single balancing act, slicing the glass-green water as it lifted and curled with the force of the planet's rotation behind him. There was no bigger rush.

Trace drove them to Twelfth Street Beach where they always went since it made a fair halfway point between homes. Also, it was less crowded. Most South Beach surfers preferred South Pointe Park where a man-made peninsula of boulders helped push the waves into bigger barrels, or at least as big as they got in Miami. The Caribbean Straight blocked most of the stronger ocean currents, so only storms brought decent waves.

Today there was no storm, so Trace and Enrique spent most of the remaining sunlight sitting atop their boards, adrift.

"My wife's leaving me," Enrique said to the water.

Trace laughed though he didn't mean to. "Hasn't she told you that before?"

"She's for real this time. Remember the girl I was with on New Year's Eve?"

"I already assumed she wasn't your wife."

"I'm in love with this girl, Trace. And now my wife is going to divorce me and take every last cent I have, and I'll be nothing, man. I'll have no one."

"You saw this coming, didn't you?"

"Not for a second."

"How did your wife even catch you?"

"Her sister saw us together. At a club. We got careless."

"So what do you want from me?"

Enrique turned his head. He hocked and spit, then cleared

his throat with a short growl, like a boat engine starting. "I want to talk about you and me taking some of the money for ourselves. A referral fee. I think we deserve it."

Trace heard a buzzing noise. He looked off over the ocean to see a low-flying Cessna airplane air-dragging an advertisement banner. For an absurd moment, he thought the model in the ad actually, impossibly, was Cassie, his ex-fiancée. The girl in the banner held a bottle of sunscreen and smiled rapturously. But it wasn't her. It couldn't be. Life didn't happen that way.

Months ago, after getting cold feet, Trace had suggested a small break in their engagement. That same night, Cassie was speeding in her Porsche down I-95 when she drunkenly got into a drag race with the traffic around her. She lost control of her car, crossed lanes, and broadsided two other cars. The accident left her with a major concussion, and a large gash running from her left temple to the opposite cheek. Numerous smaller cuts crisscrossed her chin. To fix the scars, she'd had two operations but needed more. Her modeling career was finished. She filed a lawsuit against the other driver and against the city of Miami but vanished before a hearing could even be set.

Trace understood that breaking up with Cassie had been the largest blunder of his life. Out of nowhere, he'd become hesitative in his devotion. Though he'd understood when he proposed to her that marriage meant forever, he'd never bothered to ponder what exactly forever meant. He had so much forever left to go. They both did. They were committing to something far larger than both of them. If they still wanted to get married after their break, then they both could be assured it was truly the smartest thing to do. Made sense, right?

After finally getting up the nerve, he broke it to her gently in a restaurant with soft lighting, though the lighting ended up useless. Cassie was livid.

"I've given you every ounce of love I have!" he would never forget her yelling. She even got to her feet, as if to make sure the entire restaurant heard her: "Most guys would *kill* to have a girl love them as much as I love you! And I've been *good* to you! I've bent over backwards to be a *good* girlfriend to you! And what do I get? I get put on hold while you make extra sure there aren't any better lays out there?"

The more he tried to console her and explain himself, the more upset she became until eventually she let loose with a series of overhand slaps, most landing hard against his head and forearms. She abandoned him at the restaurant before promptly crashing her car.

He hadn't seen or spoken to her since. The last anyone knew of her, she was squatting abandoned houses in London. There were even prostitution rumors. All of this happened less than four months later, mortifying Trace to his core. How could so much have gone so bad so quickly? The last thing he'd ever wanted was to demolish her life. However, there was no way around the fact that this was precisely what he'd done.

With this extra cash, he could track her down, fund all the plastic surgery her heart desired. Get her back to her parents at least. He could find her a place to live even, anything to gauze his conscious of the whole nightmare. What had become of Cassie chewed at him night and day. Trace understood he was not a good person, which was another reason he'd once felt so close to Drexel. Drexel made Trace feel good in comparison. This was becoming increasingly clear to him.

As for Drexel, if he'd actually done something to cost someone their actual life, then it was justice that he pay a price. It would be the best scenario Drexel could have because he couldn't keep running away. The worst part was, sooner or later, Drexel would discover who had done him in, and Trace would have to live with that—knowing Drexel knew. Trace also understood he could expect a trip to the witness stand. Of this, he was sure. He would have to testify that that was indeed his tape recorder and, no, he did not secretly pay a bunch of money for his friend's girlfriend to secretly record him. *Just did it because I felt it was my duty to doom him, friend or no.*

Trace had enough guilt to deal with. Enough for centuries. Though Drexel had once become more of a presence in

Trace's life than Trace was comfortable with, he didn't think he could ever betray him like this. They'd been through a lot together. And, were the roles reversed, Drexel would *never* do this to him.

"Can you give me more time to think this over?" Trace asked his partner, though he didn't need any. He'd decided he couldn't go through with it. He only wanted time now to catch his breath. Stop his mind from twirling.

"Sure," said Enrique. "Think it over."

"How long you giving me?"

"About a minute? Seriously, we need her to record him as soon as possible," Enrique explained. "Tonight would be ideal."

Pressured by the time limit, Trace found himself spending the minute, thinking more. The Cessna was making another pass and, this time, he could see for sure that the model was not Cassie.

There was always the chance Drexel could be found innocent. Or, more likely, he wouldn't confess anything to Ophelia. Otherwise, perhaps Trace could use part of the money to help bail Drexel out? That much money could solve a lot of problems. Might make Trace a good person. "You sure about this?" Trace asked.

"I would do anything for this girl. Anything."

"I guess I know the feeling."

"When he handed me that suitcase today, and I opened it...I don't know. A light went on inside me."

"A light."

"I need money, Trace."

"How much are you thinking we should take?"

"Fifty for me, fifty for you?"

"This is my good friend we're talking about."

"Tell you what. Let's go back to the bank tomorrow morning. Count that cash again. I believe you need to feel it in your hands yourself."

"Not necessary."

"So we're on the same page?"

"What if she says no?"

"You can charm her. I have faith in you."

At the shoreline, an unattended toddler sat crying before the mother scooped it up. Night edged closer. Babies were born and people died. Behind the two detectives, a slow roll of water swelled towards them. Trace almost didn't see it in time.

"Hey hey hey!" he shouted. "Here we are. We've got one. Go!"

12

It was her second time ever in Ms. Taylor's office and Ophelia could not stop her knee from bouncing. She sat in a pony-hide canvas chair, one of two, the left one. Framed prints of Allison Taylor, Inc.'s successes checkered the office walls. Ophelia saw herself there in the lower right corner. In the photo, she was still leaning over a bathroom sink, applying the acotine beneath her eyes.

Allison Taylor sat looking at an opened file folder on her desk. From what Ophelia could see without sitting up, there was a single sheet of paper inside with tiny print on it.

"Ophelia Lake," Ms. Taylor said.

"Yes, ma'am," Ophelia answered, soft and neutral.

Allison Taylor's eyes clicked up at her. "Darling, I'm afraid I have some bad news."

"You're dropping me."

"Please, try not to take it hard."

"What did you hear? I'm not the one in trouble! Drexel is!"

Ophelia had come across the story on Facebook, described in three different links. Drexel had given drugs to some mega-rich girl and she croaked, just as Ophelia thought. Crystal meth with acotine, though no one apparently knew about the acotine part. The authorities were calling for Drexel to turn himself in.

Allison Taylor lowered her eyes to the folder again and seemed to read what she said from there: "At the beginning of every year, my associates and I go over some numbers, last year's compared to the one before. And to make a long story short: We simply have too many girls under us right now. When any agency starts out, they go into a signing frenzy before cutting—"

"Weeding out the losers, I know. But I worked for a British wedding catalog, like yesterday! They said they wanted me again for next year's issue! They loved me!"

"Hon, this is something every agency goes through sooner or later. Bottom line: It's a business."

"This is because of my boyfriend. About the girl who died! I know it is."

"Listen, I'm sure you'll have little problem getting picked up elsewhere. Otherwise, you can always come see us next season."

"Well," Ophelia's voice wilted, her eyes beginning to moisten, "what if I promise to lose more weight? Or cut my hair again? I'll go to more castings!"

"You're not listening." Allison Taylor let the glasses drop and they dangled from their chain around her neck. She folded her hands on her desk. "There are tons of beautiful girls in the world. We cannot support them all. I'm sorry. You're still an extremely pretty girl and I wish you the best."

Ophelia rose slowly to her feet. What the hell was she going to do now? No man would want her anymore. Her friends would shun her. Destitute and alone, she would have to move back to North Florida, banished.

"If you ever need to talk to me, like for advice or for anything," Allison Taylor said, "feel free to call me. Okay?"

The fake concern on her face was infuriating. Like Ophelia was a hospital patient.

Robot-slow, she turned, opened the office door, and closed it behind her. She tried to keep from crying until she got out of the building, but only made it as far as the lobby. The first sob leapt out of her and after, as always, it was an avalanche. She let it go, listening to herself at the same time, to how pathetic she sounded, crying because she wasn't an Allison Taylor fashion model anymore. And because, in the space of a few minutes, she'd become nobody. Again. Ophelia The Bean Pole.

Ophelia Lake first met Drexel Waters while getting gas on her way to work one day, a secretarial position at her uncle's boat repair business in Lake City, Florida. Drexel was on his way to Miami Beach from Atlanta, traveling with his pop band called "Sunday's Mail." Thanks to Drexel's *BodyQuake Cologne* contract, the largest paying fee ever for a male model, the band had landed a development deal with Magma Records. As part of the deal, the record company agreed to fund their demo session at Criteria Studios, all without the company having heard one note of their music, having only seen Drexel's most recent layout in *Men's Fitness.*

When Ophelia met Drexel's eyes across the pumps, the tank of her VW Bug overflowed and sloshed gasoline onto her shoes and she couldn't have cared less. She understood now her reason for having been born was to love and care for this gorgeous angel before her. Less than a thousand words between them resulted in them lip-locked in back of the van, shooting south on I-75, so slapped-across-the-face-in-love, she felt convinced their meeting was cosmic.

Before even reaching Orlando, however, she felt overwhelming shame for not having done what she should have, which was park her car and leave a note for her parents beneath the wiper. Instead, she had to make two separate phone calls, her parents having been divorced since before she could remember.

Dad cried. Mom yelled. Pretty much as predicted, but well worth it. No more Monday through Friday Mom. No more weekend Father. No more hick friends who desired nothing more than babies and soap operas, stainless steel appliances and shopping lists. No more boyfriends who spat tobacco and never said much.

Best of all, no more church. Her father was a preacher, Southern Baptist to the bone. Every Sunday of her childhood had meant uncomfortable dresses and images of burning caves filled with giggling goblins, the images spewing from her father's outraged face. A lifetime of God had made her famished for a taste of Hell. Outlandish misbehavior which other people would only read about.

Ophelia adored her new identity. She was the girlfriend of the best-looking guy in the universe who also happened to be the lead singer of the universe's best pop band, living with him in a posh South Beach hotel called The Eden Roc. And it was fortunate she enjoyed the hotel because they spent weeks there, the band always a day away from finishing the demo and getting signed. Any day now. Tomorrow maybe. Next day, definitely.

Then it was over. A telegraph arrived from the record company's office in Los Angeles. "No thank you," was all it said.

Drexel changed after that. He became short-tempered, violent, lost interest in laughing. He ranted about how his band had been sabotaged by their producer, a former drummer from some one-hit wonder of the Sixties. The dude didn't know dick about making records, even if he *had* worked with Gloria Estefan.

Though Ophelia never said anything, she knew what she knew: There were plenty of people at fault, plenty of things to blame. She knew what she knew: tasting Hell was going to cost her.

While Drexel worked European runway shows, Ophelia worked as a cocktail waitress at an Ocean Drive salsa establishment known as "Coconuts." That is, until the work night when a paunchy, bearded man sprung from around his table and planted himself in front of her. He gave her his card and asked her if she'd ever thought about modeling. Because if she hadn't, then she certainly should.

He suggested she give him a call and when she did, he confettied promises at her like they were on sale, told her about how much money she could make, about traveling to Europe, about fame.

She couldn't believe it. *Her?* A fashion model? Doing the exciting stuff Drexel got to do? The once flat-chested, four-eyed Ophelia Lake, the one kids in junior high school had given the preposterous name of "Bean Pole" to, now a woman whose looks could allure people into purchasing the clothes she wore? The makeup? The newest release of some musical group?

The next morning, she found herself standing in the office of a sharp-dressed, middle-aged woman wearing frameless glasses, her face weathered in a refined sort of way. Her name was Allison Taylor and she owned the agency that the modeling scout worked for.

"How old are you, hon?" Allison Taylor asked her.

"Eighteen."

"How tall are you?"

"Six-one?"

"You're five-eleven at most."

Allison Taylor asked Ophelia to drop her skirt. While Ophelia stood immobile with uncertainty, Allison Taylor got a roll of measuring tape from her desk's top drawer. She walked to Ophelia and told her not to be shy, just drop the skirt. After Ophelia did so, Allison Taylor bent behind her and stretched the measuring tape across her ass. Allison Taylor folded her arms over her knee, considering.

"Lose about nine pounds," she said. "We'll talk."

When Ophelia lamented to a friend about the hardship of this, the friend assured her there was nothing to worry about. Cocaine was great for killing appetites. It was expensive but worth it. Cocaine made her feel juiced, ambitious, full of love and agreement. Bliss Powder.

She dropped fifteen pounds in three weeks. The cocaine also helped her combat any weaknesses she felt, which she did often, gnawing at her core, a settling decay as if some toxic ointment were invading her bloodstream, sludging it.

She went back to see Allison Taylor. A month later, Ophelia landed the acotine editorial in *Couteur Girl Magazine*. The pay for a single, twelve-hour shoot allowed her to quit her waitress job. No more frantic, horn-driven salsa blasting her world while she took drink orders from giddy, sunburnt tourists. Never again would she have to listen to Drexel casually list the countries he'd been to. Now she'd be there too.

However, turned out she only made big money from photo jobs here and there, mostly catalog work, but with the exorbitant cost of food, drugs, and clothing in Europe, she returned to South Beach broke and with no new jobs lined up.

Allison Taylor explained that it took patience at the beginning. Overnight careers were rare. Apparently, the editorial had been a fluke. Ophelia tried everything to increase her odds, even braving her fear of needles to purchase collagen lip injections. Next were breast implants Allison Taylor suggested, then financed, still encouraged by her earlier success. Ophelia dyed her hair black, then red, then orange, now blonde. Nothing helped. Few clients hired her. Most casting calls were long waits for nothing.

Of course she tried asking for Drexel's help, but ever since getting arrested, his career had predictably stalled. Drexel's "bad boy" brand became tasteless once partnered with an underage sex scandal. He was garbage.

She'd never needed his help before anyway. Maybe she wasn't pretty enough. Maybe her look was over with. Maybe there were a million Ophelias already. Billions of them. Infinity Ophelias.

13

Gary Nash sat beside his wife's hospital bed in St. Regis and marveled at how dead she already looked. She wore a transparent-green mask over her lower face. A tube extended from her mouth and into a metallic box machine. He reached over to try and wake her. Useless, he knew, but he couldn't help himself. He shook her shoulder. Shook it harder. No, she definitely didn't seem alive, despite the cardiographic blips on the heart machine indicating otherwise. He said her name. He said it louder.

"*Blip...blip, blip...*," the machine said.

The wind picked up outside, tossing snow and ice against the window, next to which lay another patient. Nash couldn't see if Carol's roommate was a man or a woman. The lights were off, so he could make out nothing but legs beneath a bedsheet. Why was his wife being forced to share a room? Didn't this hospital understand who she was? Nothing made sense anymore.

Nash touched his wife's face and was surprised to find how warm she felt. Feverish even. "Why'd you do this, Carol, huh?" he asked her.

She was the perfect companion, always had been. She kicked him in the butt when he needed it and shut her mouth when a situation didn't want words. Nash didn't mind confessing that he was not the same man without her. Not even half.

"You did this to yourself, didn't you?" he asked her. "You were a drug addict, too?"

When he'd first met Carol, she seemed baffled as to how a guy who could have any girl he wanted could choose her. Their relationship would never work. Never, except July would be their thirtieth wedding anniversary. They were the perfect balance to each other. While she wanted everything done now, right now (*"What are you waiting for? It's been two seconds already."*), Nash placed more importance on doing the research and picking the right moment. Both approaches had their pros and cons, so they made a good team. Who would he be without her?

The wind grew gustier. Shadows of the rapidly falling snow cast a staticky blanket over the roommate's bed. The storm was supposed to let up by the afternoon. Nash hoped as much. He planned on being back in Miami by that evening. Next morning the latest. He knew how odd it would appear to loved ones and to the media that he hadn't remained at his wife's bedside, but there wasn't time. Procrastination = the death of opportunity.

Besides, his daughter's body had already made the flight with him, so that particular business was finished. Her remains now rested with Manhattan Funeral Chapel in the Upper East Side, awaiting disposal. Her funeral would be Monday.

"Carol!" he shouted. "Wake up, Carol. Let's go, huh?"

Within a rounded screen, a slow, flowing, line of green light continued to graph the steady but jagged rhythm of his wife's heart. *Blip...blip, blip...*

Nash stood to kiss her and his vision filled with a succession of blinding flashes. He shielded his eyes with his left hand, disoriented. Nash crouched before realizing the flashes came from the other patient in the room. The patient was sitting up with a camera, snapping away.

"Get out of here!" Nash yelled. "You heartless asshole, get out!"

Nash rounded Carol's bed, meeting the photographer

there who continued shooting. More enraged with every flash, Nash reached for the camera. The photographer moved it to avoid Nash's grasp, but kept taking pictures, except now at the ceiling.

Blip...blip, blip...

There was a click in Nash's mind. Dial tone. He told Holly about wanting to see her again. Have one more of their coy chats at the breakfast table. That was it. One more meal. Haven't been able to stop thinking about you. Ending didn't feel like an ending. Too abrupt. Too final. Please. How about it? Just once more. Somehow. It's all I'm asking. I wish I could make you understand. It's been so hard, so thoroughly, impossibly hard. I only need someone to be my friend. Where are all my friends?

Nash's hands closed around the photographer's neck. It was too dark to see the man's face, and this made Nash squeeze harder. Nothing else would make the flashes stop. The photographer dropped the camera and it smacked the floor, banging open, the lens coming free and skidding beneath Carol's bed. The photographer clawed at Nash's hands while they crushed his jugular. He made a wheezing noise which faded.

Nash could see the man's eyes as they rolled white. His knees folded, and he went limp. Nash wouldn't let go. He couldn't, didn't, forcing every ounce of misery and anger into the strength of his grip. When he finally relaxed his hands, the photographer collapsed to the floor, a sack of potatoes.

Numb, exhilarated, horrified, then sober, catching his breath, Nash took his phone from his suit pocket, dialed his assistant Sara.

"Got that flight back to Miami yet?" he asked her.

She told him there was a problem. Blizzard had the airports closed. Didn't he get her messages?

Blip...blip, blip...

"Figure out something else then," he ordered. "I'll take off from the damn interstate if I have to. Get me back down there! Now!"

14

The hotel room resembled a ragged cage, the walls striped with darkness and moonlight. Having just arrived, Ophelia sat next to where Drexel lay on the bed. She stiffened her body and fell back across his legs.

"I've had the worst day." She situated her body alongside his. She took one of his arms and placed it around her waist.

Drexel stood from the bed and scratched his stomach. "Change your clothes. We're going out."

"Did you meet up with your friend today? The detective?"

"I did."

"And?"

"Everything is cool."

"You sure?"

"Don't worry about it."

"I got fired from my agency today because of you. I'm worried about it."

"Know what'd be awesome? Wear that black one piece. With the slits down the side."

She lifted onto her elbows. "Did you hear what I said?"

He went to the light switch and flicked it on. "That agency sucks anyway. I'll call some friends for you. It's all good."

"What's going on with you? For real. Tell me what happened between you and that girl who died."

"Stop stressing me and change your clothes." He unbuttoned his cargo shorts. *Her* cargo shorts, she noticed. He stepped out of them and arrived at her dresser. He grabbed something from there and tossed it to her.

"Catch," he said. "Snort your booger sugar if it'll get you motivated. I had some before you got here. What's wrong?"

Ophelia held the baggie away from herself. The baggie was empty except for the faintest frosting of cocaine whiting its lower sides. "You're out of control," she said.

"I'll buy you more."

"I got this yesterday!"

"I left you some."

"Know how much this cost me? And look. *Look!* There's nothing left."

"You're talking like such an addict. I wish you could hear yourself."

Ophelia stretched to the other side of the bed and took a gossip magazine from the floor. She shook out the baggie's feeble remnants over a Miami skyline picture on the magazine's cover. Blue, multi-eyed skyscrapers serrated a lava-colored sky, mirrored upside-down in the rippled, indigo water of Biscayne Bay.

"You don't even care what happened to me today," she said. "You don't even care that a person is dead."

"Why aren't you getting dressed?"

"Allison Taylor called me into her office, then said she couldn't afford losers like me anymore, so go die somewhere."

"She said that?"

"It was because of you! Everyone knows about what happened, Drexel. You've made me an outcast!"

"Find another agency. Jesus, it's not the end of the world."

Ophelia covered her face with her hands. "One day I'm going to die, and nobody'll care."

"I'll have to find a new girlfriend who can afford to take care of me." He laughed. She didn't. He walked over and slapped her arm. "Hey! Laugh! Stop being a bitch already."

Her legs parted from the impact and the magazine sank between her knees. She retightened them, but not before the book finished falling. "Drexel! Dammit!"

He leaned over, saw the aftermath. "Oops. We'll get more. Get dressed."

She slid onto her knees and elbows and inspected the carpet with her fingers. She combed what she could into the palm of her hand. "What a banner day. I love my life."

Drexel pulled on his 666 shirt, the same one he'd been wearing since New Year's. He stood and watched her. After a few minutes, he said, "Ophelia, get up. You look ridiculous. We're going out."

"Then fuck off and go. Go to hell while you're at it."

She felt him still watching her as she continued. From the corner of her eye, she saw him scratch his stomach again, cradle his crotch with the same hand. She looked up and, for the first time since she'd come in, gave his appearance her full attention. He appeared frazzled, like he'd just walked off a battlefield, an eyewitness to the unspeakable atrocities of war. His eyes were carbonated specs, ringed in shadow. She noticed he'd removed the band-aid from his unshaven neck. The cut had scabbed already.

"I lied," he said. "I didn't really see my friend today."

"Figures. I can tell when you're lying."

"It's complicated. The whole thing. The chick's father is super rich...and powerful. And I don't know what I'm going to do."

"So let's talk about this. Think of something."

"Nope. I'm going out. They'll take me down sooner or later anyway. Might as well enjoy myself while I can."

"Enjoy yourself," she repeated flatly. Using the bed for support, Ophelia got to her feet. She went to her dresser and began scanning its surface for nothing in particular.

"With me being on probation," he continued, "no matter what I say to the police or Trace or anybody, it's still fucked that I was even at the same party, much less in the same room. And

I'm supposed to meet with my probation officer this Wednesday..."

"Have you seen my lizard earrings?" She opened the oak jewelry box her father had given her and there, atop a strangled ball of necklaces, were the earrings. She scooted them deeper into the box until she could no longer see them.

"I might need you to cover for me, okay?" he said. "You wouldn't mind, would you? I don't know what else to do, babe. I am *not* going to jail again. I'd rather they kill me first."

She grabbed the jewelry box and spun with it. The box struck the wall a foot from his head. It rolled from the wall to the bed to the floor, losing its silver and gold contents behind it.

Drexel flinched, holding his hands up, braced for more missiles. When he saw none coming, he raced over to her and clutched her wrists together. "The hell was that? You could've bashed my head in!"

She went to speak but began sobbing instead.

He yelled at her: "I ask for your help and that's what I get? You chuck something at me? Last night, you try to cut my head off, and now *this?*"

She turned her head and his voice stuffed her left ear. For an endless instant, she struggled for the breath to speak. She closed her eyes.

"I hate you," she said. "I hate you so much. How can you do this to me? You fucked some little sixteen-year old and I stood by you because I forgave you and because I know everyone makes mistakes, and this is what you go and do? You're going to put me through *this*, too?"

"What are you crying for? *I'm* the one who could go to prison. Stop crying! Ophelia, I mean it!"

He made as if to hit her and she threw her arms over her head. She stumbled against her dresser.

"Ha! Look at you," he said. "How stupid. What did I ever see in you?"

He grabbed both her shoulders and she whimpered, still sobbing, sucking in breath through her teeth.

"I wish I'd never met you," Drexel kept on, "Allison Taylor doesn't even want you. The shittiest of the shitty modeling agencies. Know why? Because you're more trouble than you're worth. If you hadn't given me those shitty drugs, then gotten mad over nothing, and left me alone that night, none of this would be happening to me! Ever considered that?"

"Shut up,...leave, please...I can't..." She continued leaning back until she almost toppled. She caught herself against the wall. Her rear knocked over hairspray and perfume bottles. A lava lamp. A fat hairbrush tumbled to the floor. A magazine. She couldn't stop crying. Her face shone with tears and snot.

"Listen to you: *Boo-hoo. Boo-hoo,*" he mimicked. He made an exaggerated sobby face at her. "*Boo-hoooooo...Liddle, widdle crybaby...Boo-hoooooo...*"

He shoved her.

She screamed. She touched her elbows before her face and lay almost completely across the dresser.

A knock at the door. "Everything okay in there? We're getting complaints!" It was hotel staff.

Drexel backed off and allowed her feet to retouch the carpet.

Ophelia coughed and sniffed. "It's okay!" she called back shakily. "We're just playing around!"

They stared at the door and waited for a reply. When there was none, he turned back to her.

"Don't you think I feel bad, too?" he whispered. "Ophelia, I'm sorry. I didn't know the girl was going to overdose." With his thumb, he wiped away dots of his saliva from her cheek. "Anyway, I need to go somewhere for a while. Disappear. I'm sure Trace knows I'm hiding here. I've even been half-expecting SWAT to bust through the door or come swinging through the window."

Ophelia eased her arms down, but kept her head turned... *Don't look at him. Let him say whatever he was going to say, but make him go...Make him go...Don't look...*

"I don't know," he said. "I have to think about this. What

I'm going to do. I have to go out."

She tucked her lips in and swallowed.

His hand slid beneath her hair and cupped the back of her head. "Whatever I decide though, I want you to do it with me. Maybe we'll leave the country. The two of us. You're not doing anything better, right? We can disappear together easy. It'd even be kind of fun, wouldn't it? Like, an adventure."

...Don't look. Make him go...Make him...Don't...

"Ophelia, dammit, come on. Everything's going to be all right. I promise. I said I was sorry. I'm an asshole. What else do you want me to say?"

With two fingers Drexel forced the corners of her mouth into a smile. Her smile disappeared when he took his fingers away.

He said, "I hate this has happened. But this is the way things are now. We have to keep thinking positive, and we'll make it through this. You still love me, don't you? Hey – you love me?"

She wiped her eyes with her wrists. She nodded.

He placed a hand over her breast and pushed it in with his palm. "Mad?"

She surprised herself by nodding. She removed his hand. "I need to be alone. Just, Drexel, just a little while. I need to...I need quiet."

He stepped back and tugged on his pants. It took a few hops to get them on. He buttoned them. "You want to be alone? Sure. Your call. I'll leave you alone. No problem."

As he strapped on his shoes, Ophelia grew transfixed with the star design on his Canvas sneakers, white within – what was that? Maroon?

He said, "Stay put and take it easy. I'll leave you alone to think about what you want to do. I love you."

She sniffled hard. "Um, yeah, come back later or something."

"It stung when you said you hated me. You didn't mean it, did you? You hate me?"

"Me?" She shook her head. "No."

"Don't hate me. Not you, too. Anything but that." He lifted her chin with his finger. "See you later, Mutilator?"

He told her he'd give her a call from somewhere. Drexel opened the door and, impossibly, was gone.

Afterwards, the empty room continued shouting at her. The alarm clock by her bed blinked 12:00. She wondered if the clock had become unplugged somehow or if the electricity had gone off during the afternoon.

Lord, help me. I'm coming apart. Forgive me for what I'm about to do.

Ophelia curled up on the bed and dozed off. She dreamed she was in an old Super 8 home movie, a netherworld where motion was sped up, making everyone seem witlessly hyper and nervous. The lighting was stark and shaky, and it rained black and yellow spots. There was no sound, the dream holding no voice but the gurgle and purr of a film projector.

She dreamed she was two years old again, playing in a kiddy pool while her mother sat in a nearby lawn chair. They were in the backyard of their rusted trailer in Lake City, Florida. Ophelia stirred her fist against the surface of the water, imperiously demanding something.

She dreamed of the time she stood on the balcony of a Mexican hotel. Her and Drexel were in Cancun, a romantic weekend away together. She sat in a chair to his right while he applied lotion to his sunburnt face. He yawned and his mouth opened so wide, she feared his head might swallow itself.

She dreamed she stood again in the backyard of her old home. Family cookout. She worked at extricating a long, gooey rope of gum from her hair while her older brother and his friends laughed uproariously from across the yard.

She dreamed she was running down a tunnel of tall trees, milky rays of sunlight crisscrossing down through the branches, creating a lane littered with glowing pools, showing her the way as she ran and ran and ran from the darkness behind her...

She heard the hotel phone from far away. Ophelia remained barely aware she was even having a conversation until she hung up and felt the physical reality of the receiver in her hand, the physical reality of the cradle beneath. She arose and dressed while keeping an eye on her door, expecting Drexel to walk through at any second.

It was Trace who called, the detective. He asked about Drexel and she told him he'd left, and she didn't know where he'd gone or when he would be back. She agreed to meet Trace in an hour, even though it was pouring rain.

"If you'd like to make a call," the phone told her, "please, hang up and try again. If you need help, hang up, and then dial your operator."

Meeting up with Trace was what her plan called for anyway. But she also needed somewhere else to go. Someone else to be with. Someone safe. In a safe place. Before Drexel got back.

She sat holding the phone.

"*Eh! Eh! Eh! Eh! Eh! Eh! Eh! Eh! Eh! Eh!*" the phone said.

Nash awaited his private jet to finish taxing the runway at Teterboro Airport. Snow fell in gusty, gray torrents, yet the runway remained clear, the noisy work of a building-sized snowplow. Its extra-wide plow made it resemble a giant orange beetle.

Nash remained fixated on the vehicle until his cell buzzed. It was Sara, his assistant, winded from the stress of finding Nash a plane to Miami in a blizzard.

"Listen," she said, "I'm so sorry about Carol, okay? I swear! And Holly! You must be—"

"Everything's under control, Sara," he assured her. "I can control this."

"Do you want me to fly down there with you? I'll do it.

Just tell me. I was actually able to find two planes."

The pilot asked Nash to please put his seatbelt on. They were taking off soon.

"Fuck your seatbelt," Nash informed him. "Get us into the damn sky!"

"Are you talking to me?" Sara asked.

"No, sweetie," he said. "Sorry."

"I seriously need you to put on your seatbelt, sir," said the pilot without turning around. He focused on a clipboard he held. "This is some crazy heavy wind. Are you religious?"

"If I tell you 'yes,' can we please fly?"

"You're the boss. We're doing it. Put your seatbelt on though."

The pilot pushed a button and this started the plane. The propellers on each wing chugged for breath before spinning into silver discs. The deafening buzz of the twin engines blended with the wind, an orchestra of howls.

15

Trace set his elbows on the bar and watched her talk. Her lipstick resembled oil, black base with a rainbow sheen. He focused on the black lips pushing out her words, the itsy-bitsy freckle riding the tip of her lip. And her teeth! So tiny. So many of them. She must have had a million of those things in there.

He managed to learn everything and nothing about Ophelia. Her parents' initial reason for having wanted a child was to receive government aid, but not that they didn't love her. Her father smoked a pipe and read lots of books and loved old, comedic movies. He knew every single word of the *Holy Bible* by heart. Her mother loved plants. She loved animals. She loved music. She sang in the shower in a reedy voice, the worst sound you'd ever want to hear.

The drinking establishment Trace and Ophelia occupied was a narrow building, sandwiched between wailing nightclubs. Since there was no charge for admission, no doorman to haggle, this particular bar was popular with blue-collar types. It was easy to enjoy the disciplined negligence of the place, succeeding at being nothing more than what it was: a sports bar. There were beer label mirrors, standing cardboard cutouts of curvy women in bikinis, sparkling with perspiration, and cradling beer bottles. There were posters of beer bottles wearing football helmets, beer bottles wearing funny hats and bandannas and toothy grins, everywhere beer bottles, their logos resembling coats of arms, something grand and old and trustworthy.

As hard as he tried to focus, Trace missed a lot of what Ophelia's mouth said, its voice drowned out by the other shouted conversations around them. Or someone would press against his back while trying to get the bartender's attention. Or an attacking mist of perfume would stab his brain at the place where his spine screwed in.

"You probably want to know why I asked you here," he finally said.

"I figured you'd tell me when you were ready."

He searched the ceiling, stalactited with NFL Football banners. "I need a special favor from you," he said. He shifted on his stool, crossed his arms. "Would you be willing to tape some of your conversations with Drexel? This girl's father is willing to pay you."

"You want me to wear a wire? Like in the movies?"

"This man is offering to pay you extremely well. He wants to nail Drexel pretty bad."

"And you're okay with this? Aren't you his friend?"

"Drexel needs help."

"So help him."

"This is the help."

"Putting him away in prison?"

"He won't go to prison. I doubt it. Not for too long."

He waited while she finished her word selection. "How much money are we talking about?" she asked.

"Hundred grand."

Ophelia winced, sucked her breath. "I don't know. I don't think so."

Trace soaked a few seconds in what she'd said. He replied, "Okay," though he didn't actually know if it was.

"I could never do that to him," she said. She looked straight ahead, her forehead in her hand. "Not for every dollar in the world actually."

The tension melted from his shoulders. He shook his head. "Will you at least think about it?"

"It'll probably cross my mind again, sure."

Trace finished his beer. He set it down and scooted the bottle forward on the bar. "Drexel's pretty lucky to have a girl like you."

She half-smiled, shrugged. "Okay."

"Look, I'm going to the restroom. When I get back, we'll talk about something else, all right? Anything."

"Promise?"

He set a twenty on the bar and pushed it up next to his empty bottle. "Here. For two more beers."

"You keep." Ophelia pushed the twenty back at him. She took her purse from around her shoulders and unclasped its mouth. "I can pay."

There was a brief but intense debate over this.

Finally, he retrieved his money. "You'll still be here when I get back?"

"Go away, and let's see. You never know what I'll do. Girl like me."

The unmistakable acidic vapor of an alcohol-sponged body. Ophelia smelled him the microsecond before she saw him. He wore a gold and garnet-striped shirt, untucked, Docker slacks, a mild set of canvas sneakers. His hair was somewhere between blond and red without being orange. The rear was shaved skin-short, bangs long and combed back.

"Hi, what is happening?" He offered a pink, sweaty hand to her. He stood with the slack-jawed, clumsy stance of someone hammered. "My name's David...David Cook."

She shook his hand.

"What's your name?" he asked her.

"Ophelia," she answered.

"*'Delia?'* Where you from?"

"Lake City."

He pounded a palm to his chest. "I'm from New York. And I love you. You're awesome. Ever been to New York?"

"Of course."

"I came here for New Year's with some friends from NYU. This place is insane, huh? South Beach? My whole life, I've never seen this many fake people in one place. Must be something in the water, huh?"

She laughed.

Encouraged to see he could entertain her, that the conversation had lasted longer than ten seconds, David Cook roared an automatic weapon-ish laugh. "Let me ask you: the guy who was sitting here. He your boyfriend?"

"I'm not—Yes, he is."

"Excuse me, but I have to tell you something. I can't help myself." He tapped her shoulder with his knuckles. "Can I tell you something?"

She hummed inquisitively.

"My friends and I think you are absolutely the most knock-dead, ravishing,...*gorgeous* creature we have ever laid eyes on. You could stop a parade. My friends, they're sitting over there." He pointed behind him and she looked, but she couldn't tell which group of guys he could possibly be referring to. There were multitudes.

"Are you a model?" he asked her.

She sipped from her beer and nodded.

"*Gah!* What a stupid question. This is South Beach, right? And look at you. I've seen you on the cover of something. I know I have."

"I doubt it. Not in The States."

"Wait, why don't you come over and join us?"

"I'm here with someone already."

"He could join us, too. We love meeting all sorts of new people. We're super friendly. Come see."

"Not a good time."

He gave her a light tug. "Aww, not even for two seconds? Don't be a snob. You'll love us."

"I am sorry, no. I can't."

"*Mademoiselle*, can I at least buy you a drink?" He placed a hand on her shoulder, squeezed it hard.

"Ow! Your hand."

He removed the hand and held a finger up. "One drink? One little, itty, bitty, harmless drink? With me? Pretty please? I'd be flattered."

"I'm good. No thank you."

He went to say more but stopped. He studied her. His face calmed, and she noticed how sweaty and red it appeared. David Cook from New York lowered his face into his hand and wiped it. He blinked a lot.

"I am totally wasting my time," he said, as though to himself. "I don't have a prayer."

"A prayer for what?" She instantly regretted asking. She knew the answer but was now going to have to hear it anyway. She noticed her hands beginning to tremble. She joined them together and laid them on the bar.

David Cook ranted as if this were a scenario ached for since adolescence: "Well, you probably don't go out with a guy unless he's a top photographer, or another model, or a celebrity, or someone who it'll help your career to be seen with, right? A mere mortal like myself would need hundred-dollar bills spilling out of my pockets, wouldn't I?"

"No, I'm sorry, you mis—"

He bent his arms up and held his hands out. "Hey, no need to apologize. I understand my place."

Over his shoulder, she spotted Trace making his way along the wall, too focused on navigating a path through all the people to notice much else.

David Cook pointed in her face. "Remember something, little Miss Brain-Dead Barbie Doll: Beauty fades. All right? You shit too, you know."

She stared at him in open-mouthed dismay. Her voice

came raspy and thin: "That was a good one. You win. You can walk away now."

"Y'know, up close, you're not as pretty as I thought you were."

Having lost sight of him, she cried out in surprise when he appeared. Trace grabbed the boy's finger and jerked it up. Trace asked what the hell and he was elbowed in the eye. Ophelia watched from another world away as Trace punched the boy's face. He fell and grabbed Trace's belt loops on the way down. They rolled together on the floor, struggling. As soon as it had started, the fight was over. Trace and David Cook from New York became head-locked by bouncers, yanked to their feet, then hustled towards the exit.

For a silly, inexplicable moment, Ophelia couldn't decide what to do with her purse. Her mind locked on the pointless crisis of whether to put it around her shoulder or simply hold it. She looped her purse over her shoulder and weaved her way after him.

Trace sat hunched over at the end of Ophelia's bed, feeling things in common with a well-chewed dog toy. His head seemed like the left side weighed more than the right. He'd received similar sensations the morning after a football game.

Ophelia entered her hotel room with a plastic bucket of ice, fetched from the machine down the hall. She entered the bathroom with it and returned with ice cubes wrapped in a washcloth.

She pressed the damp, cold bundle against his cheek. "Here. Hold it in place."

"How do I look?"

"Like you got into a fight." She wiped at his cheek. "Thanks for saving me."

"To serve and protect."

She sat next to him on the bed. "This girl's father straight-on blames Drexel for her daughter dying, huh?"

"That came from nowhere. Are you starting to change your mind?"

"No." She looked at her feet and flexed them. "I'm only thinking about how terrible the poor guy must feel. Honestly."

"My partner and I have been forced to spend time with him. He's pretty twisted up, yeah."

Ophelia shook her head slow. "I wish I had at least a drop of control over Drexel. Stop him from doing things like this. He won't stop."

Trace relocated the iced washcloth to his lip and winced. "Ow, pain pain pain pain pain..."

"Shhh." She placed a finger beneath his chin and turned his head. She guided the hand holding the cloth away from his face. She kissed the side of his mouth, which had gone numb from the ice. "Thank you again for saving me."

Trace froze. Both of them held their breath from the aftershock of her kissing him.

He opened the washcloth. The ice inside had disintegrated from cubes to smooth, watery stones. An image of Cassie flashed in his mind. She held a voodoo doll of him, windmilling her arm as she slapped the doll repeatedly against a table corner.

"Know what would make me feel better?" he asked Ophelia. Before she could answer, he said, "What you did a second ago. The thing with your lips." He flickered a finger at where she'd kissed him.

"A kiss?"

"Maybe one more?"

"Okay, but a small one. For being my hero. And because bruises are sexy."

He nodded, and she kissed him, and he made sure it was on the lips. He made sure it wasn't small.

When the kiss was over, she leaned her head against his chest and spread her hand on his stomach. "What in the world?"

"I know. This is destructive and thoughtless and selfish, and I don't even care. I want you. A lot."

She sat back from him. "It's pretty wrong."

He reached behind her, fumbled briefly for her dress' zipper before easing the zipper downwards.

She dropped her shoulders, so the top of her dress slipped off into her lap. She held his eyes as she undid her bra. Ophelia reached around his neck and pulled him towards her. They kissed hard, mouths open and biting.

She lay back across the bed, arching her body, pulling off her dress. She wedged a hand inside her panties. Trace watched as she appeared to use two fingers for scissoring her clit before working the fingers inside.

"This might sound weird," she said to Trace. She looked down at her busy hand. She gasped, exhaled, winced. "But I really want you...to do it. I've wanted it...ever since I met you."

Trace was in the process of kicking off his pants. "You have my attention."

"Tell me to show you my pussy. Say that you want to see me."

Trace removed his underwear. "I want to see you."

"Say it."

He touched himself, stroking slow. "Show me your pussy," he said. "Open your legs and show it to me."

Ophelia slid off her panties while keeping her hips turned. "Come over here," she told him.

Trace stepped closer and placed himself between her legs, still standing. "Show me your pussy," he whispered.

She hid herself with her hands while rocking her knees back and forth. "I don't know. Maybe not. I'm shy."

"Dammit, show me your pussy." Trace swallowed, his breath shallow. "Show it to me."

She rocked her knees a while longer before gradually removing her hands. He saw that her mound was shaved with two wings of slight pubic hair making a V. Her pussy was tiny and tulip-shaped with small, shimmering-pink petals.

"Does that look delicious to you?" she asked him.

"It's the most beautiful thing I've ever seen." He touched

her knee, slid his hand along the inside of her leg. "I want to taste you."

This made her knees sway again. She reached down and opened herself. "Hell yeah. Eat my pussy. Do it. Stick your fingers in me, too. Deep. Everything deep."

Her phone buzzed from beside his left foot. From pure reflex, Trace glanced down and saw the screen. It was Drexel calling because of course it was. Trace used his big toe to nudge Ophelia's phone beneath the bed.

16

Nash leveled the gun at her face. He regarded Sara on the bed with a mixture of fascination and revulsion. His assistant narrowed her eyes at him.

The flight had been extra bumpy during takeoff, but the Cessna recovered fine once climbing over the storm. Nash arrived back at his hotel room, removed the gun from the safe, placed it into a calf leather duffel bag. He next found an hourly-rated motel on Biscayne Boulevard, downtown Miami, the scummiest he could find. He chose this one mainly because most of the letters in the neon signage were burned out. The sign read: "vacancy," nothing else. Sara had called and met him here within an hour of his own arrival.

"Um, what are you doing?" she asked him. She lay there in a nuclear-green rectangle of light from the "vacancy" sign, only a few feet away through the window. She wore a wool blazer and matching pencil skirt. Sara was mid-thirties, Polynesian with blond-streaked brown hair. Her heels sat side-by-side on the floor.

"Scared?" he asked her.

"I'm deciding on it." She sat up, crossed her stockinged legs. She dropped her hands and held her breath until she coughed, exhaled.

"Does it turn you on?" he asked her.

"Gary, what are we doing here?"

"I've never stayed in a motel."

"What are you talking about? You most certainly have."

"No, a hotel is different. You have to get to your room through the lobby. Motels you drive to the door."

"Well, it sucks, and it doesn't make any sense." She lay back again, an arm over her head, the other hand scratching her lower belly through her skirt. "You can put the gun down. You don't have to act like a psycho. It's okay."

"Sorry." He kept the gun steadied at her.

Wet lines oozed from the corners of Sara's eyes, yet she wasn't crying. "Why would you even think of doing that to me?"

"I heard the guy who killed my daughter has been living in a hotel on South Beach."

"You heard from *me*. *I* told you that."

"I'm going to kill him. Tonight. Right now maybe."

This turned her head. She didn't speak, and the motel room became smaller from it.

Nash went to the window, parted the curtain. A glossy-black Lincoln had been following him since the airport, but he didn't see it now. He stepped away from the window, faced her again. "Will you help me do it?"

"Will you shoot me if I don't?"

He lowered the gun. "No."

Sara gazed up at him. She bit her bottom lip. "Pay me enough, Gary, and I'll do anything. I'll kill somebody. I don't give a shit."

"How much do you want?"

She ran a hand through her hair, kept it there. "A hundred zillion."

"This isn't a joke, sweetie."

"Yes, it is! You're freaking out because you've lost your daughter. You've completely lost perspective."

"I almost killed a man last night," he said. "I choked him."

She bent a brow. "What happened?"

"Are you scared *now*?"

"Honestly, you never stop scaring me."

Nash tightened his grip on the gun, raised it once more at her. He imagined pulling the trigger, her head exploding against the wall, brains and blood dripping like pancake batter.

Sara frowned. She sat up again by swinging her legs over. "Please, stop pointing that fucking thing at me? I know you're upset but come on."

"Ten more seconds. Then never again. I promise. Just need to get used to this. Pointing a gun at someone."

She touched her throat. "Can I have something to drink at least? I'm thirsty."

He lowered the gun again, slow. "Yeah, put your shoes on and we'll go somewhere," Nash told her. "I'm thirsty, too."

Less than three miles away, Drexel was having sex with a girl he'd just met in Lummus Park. Or, more accurately, she was having sex with him. She was a Jamaican with blond pigtails going for a jog and now they were in her apartment. She'd given him shrooms but neglected to take any herself.

On a naked mattress, Drexel rolled onto his stomach, having to do the turning with his shoulders, his wrists handcuffed behind him. He lifted his ass by drawing his legs in.

The carpet blinked with millions of red eyeballs, which untangled themselves from the short-haired threads and floated upwards. They popped when they touched each other.

The girl approached him from behind. She leaned over and ran her fingernails against his skin, making white trails there which stayed. He wasn't able to see the white trails, but he knew they were there. She instructed him to say things, pornographic things.

Drexel complied. He laughed and sobbed. He couldn't tell which. He panted and his sides ached.

"Isn't this gorgeous?" the girl wanted to know. "So awesome I get to do this."

Her skin developed green scales. Her head dissolved, then transmogrified into the oversized, orbed head of a fly, her bristled, narrowed face framed by green hair. He began gnawing the pillow, gurgling, groaning, growling. Drexel tried to remember her name, but it wouldn't come to him. He became hypnotized by the staggered flight paths of yellow and blue butterflies around the bed.

The red eyeballs had disappeared. No, they hadn't.

Drexel gazed down at the room from its ceiling and was struck with the perfect name for his firstborn: Albatross. Wait, what time was it? He had to be somewhere, didn't he?

A portable CD player spoke a continuous dance beat, interspersed with people chanting, "*La ilaha illa Allah.*" Plus TV sounds, gunshots and tires screeching and anchormen mumbling from TelePrompTers. A staticky hologram twitched at the back of Drexel's brain...He saw Ophelia standing before a cliff. She beamed angelically until her hair began slithering down around her shoulders, the strands clustering into snakes which ate vigorously of her neck, chewing off fleshy, drippy portions before tunneling through her torso. She watched this happening to herself and smiled.

"Hip hip horaaayy!" the girl hollered. She didn't have a fly's head anymore. Yes, she did. She took a long length mirror from the wall and brought it closer to the bed.

Drexel could see himself, handcuffed with his ass in the air. He noticed, above the bed, radiated a poster of a drenched kitten. Its soapy hair pointed out in triangular fragments. I HATE MONDAYS, the poster read. He remembered the girl had actually told him that her name was "Tuesday." The random, corny juxtaposition of this was more than Drexel could handle. He screamed laughter.

There were dots everywhere. Eyeballs everywhere. Green penises sprouted from the walls, the walls cracking, a pig with its snout pressed against the window, a doll's head in its mouth, its breath creating foggy ovals on the glass, becoming the ovaled eyes of a white-furred werewolf who seemed like he might be friendly.

When the girl pushed him onto his side, Drexel winced and hissed. She walked over to him and took him in her hands. She guided his cock towards her face and the length of him became inhaled by the glowing cavity of her mouth, her pink, bulbous lips closing, fastening, squeezing, turning red, redder, the redness floating off her lips and getting into her hair, coating Drexel's cock, climbing his abdomen.

Punched in the stomach by another laughter convulsion, one after another, he slid off the bed. When his knees met the floor, the floor continued, around and around, faster and faster until the world became a colorful milkshake vortex which sucked him into its womb, a place where no harm should ever reach and won't for a while to come.

17

When Trace drove up on the accident scene, he had the urge to floor it, add to the pile-up. He wanted to destroy the new reality created by the phone call he'd received only fifteen minutes before. It was Cassie. Her and two other cars on I-95, just east of the airport.

Trace slid to a stop on the road's shoulder, then opened his door so violently that its springs retracted, the door knocking him into the driver seat again. He got back up, got back out, and left the door open behind him.

Two units, a fire truck, and an ambulance had already arrived. It was pouring, a flurry of red and blue rain. Two of the accident cars sat face-to-face on the road, locked in a smashed kiss, steam gushing from their radiators. The third car lay overturned in the ditch, a riviera-blue Porsche—Cassie's car.

Running to her, Trace passed two firemen unclasping a compartment within the fire truck's side. They wrestled out a hydraulic chainsaw and jogged with it behind Trace.

The Porsche's roof had been squashed even with its doors.

The bigger of the two firemen yanked the chainsaw's cord. After a few attempts, the chainsaw coughed wispy smoke bands. There came the shrill cry of metal against metal as the blade carved open the car. The fireman completed a square following the door line, blue-white sparks spurting from the incision point. He and his partner shook the door loose and away

Trace watched himself, marionetted by hysteria, push past two firemen, snatch a flashlight from the smaller one's grasp, all in the same motion. Trace submerged his elbows and knees into ditch water. He crawled inside the overturned vehicle and brushed away crumbs of glass with his hand.

The stark beam of his flashlight bloomed over Cassie's upside-down face, the eyes open but unseeing, her forehead and cheeks striped with rivulets of dark blood. Her hair lay bundled on the car's ceiling. Her expression was one of suspended concern, stuck on initial awareness, a millisecond before understanding what was about to happen.

As Trace felt her neck for a pulse, blood trailed in a thin but steady thread from her nostrils. It spilled over his wrist and dripped into a perfectly circular pool below and that was one detail which would always stay with Trace – the pool, growing, how perfectly circular it was.

The rain-beaded lens of Ophelia's hotel window made the sun appear as though it were floating in pieces.

He lifted his head as Ophelia turned hers and their faces stopped on one another.

She closed her eyes and Trace ran a thumb over her right eyelid.

"My brain," Trace whispered. "It's burning."

"You're hungover?" She licked her lips and grimaced from the taste of something vile there. "You said you'd drink me under the table."

"What else did I say? I'm drawing a blank." He considered lining his body with hers and bringing her into him, hugging her from behind, savoring that warm, charged layer between two bodies fresh from sleep.

She pulled the covers up to her throat. "What happens

now?"

"We help each other."

"I assume you mean me wearing a wire."

"Would be the best thing you could do for him."

Her face seemed to worry over another question, but all she said next was, "I kind of doubt that."

She reached for her purse and extracted a pack of cigarettes. She lit two of them at the same time, then gave him one. The swift grace with which she did this made Trace worry he might be falling in love with her.

"Is there actually something between you and me or was this to get revenge?" he asked her. He exhaled. Their smoky breath created planks of window light, which hovered over their laps.

She sucked thoughtfully on her cigarette. "How old are you?"

"Thirty-one."

"Kids?"

"Not that I'm aware."

"Married?"

"Almost. Once."

Ophelia lay back again and turned onto her side. She stared at a spot on the wall. "Why do you drink so much?"

He chuckled, taken aback. "Didn't realize I did."

"You're drinking every time I see you. If you want to escape your pain, you should smoke weed. Relax you out."

"I work for law enforcement. They tend to test us for things like that."

"They don't mind if you're an alcoholic, but being a pothead would get you fired?"

"It would get me *arrested*. Besides, drinking makes you drunk, not high. Huge difference."

"Give me one good reason pot should be illegal. I'll bet you can't."

"Well, for one, drugs make you anti-social. Anti-society. Laws were designed to keep the society together."

"And that's why you're police? You want to keep the society together?"

He considered whether or not to answer this honestly and decided, to hell with it. Maybe she'd appreciate his openness. He said, "My dad was a cop. It was just expected."

After a lengthy span of silence, Ophelia said, "I should get going."

"Something I said?"

"I have a shoot to go to."

"What time are you done?"

"Not sure. I don't know these people. They're someone Drexel set me up with." She seemed to think about this, then added: "A long time ago." She extinguished her cigarette in the nightstand's ashtray. She stood and began collecting her clothes from the floor.

"It's a lot of money, Ophelia. Think hard about my offer, okay?"

The collar of her T-shirt gave birth to her head. "I haven't stopped."

"Look, I know you could use the money. I know your agency fired you."

"You snooped on me?"

"It's job-related. Nothing personal." Trace ran his hand over the space where she'd lain. "Look, I've done everything I can for Drexel, okay?"

"Like what? Fuck his girlfriend?"

"Funny."

She lifted her hair loose from her collar and shook it out. She began dialing on her phone. "I'm calling a taxi. You can stay if you want. Drexel might even show up."

"Sounds like I better get dressed then."

She finished the clasp on her belt. She pulled here and there at her shirt to erase awkward bulges. She looked around herself. "I'm missing a sock." She moved aside the covers and got on her knees to look beneath the bed.

After putting all of his clothes on, Trace tried helping her find the missing sock. They couldn't find it.

Once he got home, Trace changed into khakis and a knitted pullover. He entered his living room where he flicked on his turntable stereo, watched the needle rise, shift over, descend. He waited for the music to start before going to the kitchen, the refrigerator, taking out a bottle of vodka and a jar of grapefruit juice. He added the remaining contents of both into a glass and stirred them with his finger. Trace downed the drink in one toss, clamping his teeth on the glass. He considered the results of taking a bite. The immense blood and agony of it.

He decided instead to think about Ophelia. He missed her already. Could even still smell her perfume a bit. Still heard her voice in his head. The delicate but warm lilt.

Trace shoved aside a stack of *Heralds* on his couch and had a seat. He fended off thoughts over what last night now meant for his situation with Drexel. Trace knew what he'd done would never be considered "tactically sound," but he couldn't help himself. Her presence disintegrated him. Even a quick-flash memory of Ophelia's naked body made colors more colorful.

The needle stuck as Frank Sinatra started the opening line of the song: "*Is it the way that I touch is it the way that I touch is it the way that I touch,*" he crooned.

18

He took Sara to a Fifties throwback diner called Munson's. It was the nearest place open at four in the morning. The diner sat in the shadow of the Miami InterContinental, a half-circle-shaped skyscraper, lit up in white, a structure Nash recognized from nearly every postcard of downtown Miami ever printed. The diner was large, sporadically seated, and quiet save for the metallic telegraph of silverware scrapping. A framed black & white of Andy Warhol sharing a booth here with Mick Jagger and Salvador Dali hung near the cash register, an event which seemed quite improbable but there it was.

Nash sat with his assistant in a booth by a large window overlooking Biscayne Boulevard, barely visible through a blob of fake cobwebs. Above them, a cardboard black cat arched its back, hair standing jagged,, mouth open in a silent shriek. Management had apparently neglected to ever remove their Halloween decorations, choosing instead to display the current holidays over top of them.

A lush but short Christmas tree stood sentient by the front door, ice-blue lights blinking slow, branches glistening with tinsel. Next to the tree sat a later-aged teenager, straddling a stool by the front door. He wore a shredded denim jacket held together with safety pins. His shiny scalp was split by a blue Mohawk, rigid as a broom brush. He drummed his lap.

"You mad at me?" Nash asked his assistant.

Sara answered by taking such a large bite of her burger that it guaranteed she wouldn't say anything else for a few minutes. For such a skinny thing, she could sure shovel the food. Nash had ordered a burger as well but cowered from the obscenely large mound of steaming fries arriving with it. His plate remained untouched in front of him.

The question hung there, waiting for her to finish chewing. Instead, Sara hummed noncommittally.

He searched for something else to say. "I'm supposed to be having a fundraiser this weekend, right? Save the whales? Or the orphans? The rain forest? I don't remember."

She swallowed finally and said, "Fuck it, huh?"

The punk-haired teenager by the Christmas tree slumped to his knees, then to his face. He lay there spread-eagle, as though having fallen from a tremendous height. Two waiters approached the punk boy and bent over him. One of the waiters slapped him and laughed. Nash overheard the word "ambulance."

Nash turned his head back around from looking. "But you spent so much time organizing everything," he said to her.

"This is what you're worried about now?"

"I guess not."

"What are you hoping to gain from offing this guy anyway?"

"Satisfaction. Justice. Some people need killing." He noticed the sun was coming up. Traffic grew heavier. It felt hot already. One of those bright Miami mornings threatening to dissolve everything. Nash spotted the black Lincoln parked across the street, the same one as before. He remembered it for its spotlessness and a long antenna atop the rear trunk. Nash was definitely being followed. "Sometimes there's no other way," he said, still looking out the window. "I deserve my revenge, don't I?"

"Do you?" Sara watched him, waiting to hear more. When he didn't elaborate, she sighed at the table. "Mind if I order dessert? I'm ordering dessert." She took the laminated, plastic menu from the seat beside her and opened it, the pages large as any world map. "Hey, this menu says I can get cheesecake *a la mode*. What does '*a la mode*' mean?"

"It means 'with ice cream.' How could someone who works for me not know that?"

Sara slapped the table, hard enough to even turn a few heads from the tragedy unfolding at the diner's entrance. She grinned triumphantly. "How about that? '*A la mode.*' Sounds like poetry!"

"Are you going to help me do this or not?"

She returned to her menu. "Don't you already know people who could take care of this for you?"

"Nope."

A crowd had gathered around the punk boy. The waiters turned him onto his back where he began convulsing. His shoulders vibrated against the floor while the foamy corners of his mouth spilled over.

"Dear Jesus," Sara said, "why is that happening? Bad energy everywhere."

"I have no one else left to help me," he told her. "You have this in you, Sara. I know you do."

"You don't know anything. I'm just expendable. What a perfect way to get rid of me, huh?"

"Give me some credit. That's nuts."

Sara finished her Coke through her straw, making a slurping sound like a shower drain struggling. With the straw still in her mouth, she said, "Let's go back to the hotel. There's something we should do. Something you need badly."

Nash straightened. "Like what?"

"You know what I'm referring to."

"But I've already adjusted my pain." He threw his napkin on the table. "It's the only reason I can walk and talk right now."

Sara sat up, lifted the same napkin. She wiped her mouth with it. "It's what you need," she said. "You need to let out some psychic steam. *A la mode* for your soul, Gary."

◆ ◆ ◆

A quilt-work of tattoos sheathed Sara's nude body. She hid them so well beneath her clothes, that seeing her undressed drove his libido through the roof of outer space, as if there were a completely different person inside the woman who worked for him. A secret she-devil behind the straight business. Her tattoos included an actual-sized heart stabbed with stars and dripping blood to her navel. Two Chinese dragons spiraled from her waist to the front of her shoulders, exhaling sharp, orange flames, which coated her upper arms on all sides. A scarlet lasso of tangled serpents wrapped her waist. Her thigh held a spider-web, its spider resting on her thigh, dangling by a thin and black line.

Nash stood in the living room of his suite, curtains wide-open, displaying a backdrop of endless, horizonless dark. He was nude himself, wrists handcuffed together above his head, with chains attached to the cuffs, the chain's other end attached to a sprinkler head. This seemed like a fairly easy contraption to pull free from, but when he gave it a good pull there was no give whatsoever. He understood pulling harder would likely result in the sprinkler coming free, flooding the room with well water. He considered doing it, just to do it, but didn't.

"When Carol and I first got married," Nash said to Sara, "we made love five times a week, rain or shine. But it didn't matter. I still jerked off like crazy. And not just normal hiding-in-the-bathroom stuff."

"I know about your issues," Sara stated blankly. She was far more focused on what she was doing to the skin of his back.

Nash continued: "I used to tie myself up naked with a power cord, or any sort of rope I could get my hands on, tied tight until it hurt."

"You're going to make me stab you if you don't hold still," she said from behind him.

"One night I was naked on my bed with an orange extension cord," he kept on. "I'd taken the cord from the garage and wrapped it all around my body and I was jerking off. It was like ten o'clock at night, maybe later."

"Is this hurting you yet?" she asked him.

He still kept on, though it seemed he was talking to himself: "Somehow I forgot to lock my door and in walks the maid. I don't remember her name. She even used to work for my father. And there we were, me and this woman from Guatemala, staring at each other, neither of us quite believing what we're seeing. A minute went by and she said, 'Everything is cleaned,' and I said, 'Okay,' and she said, 'And Ophelia isn't home yet',' and I said, 'Thanks,' and she shut the door and that was it." Subtle at first, a distant sting before electric ants scurried through his arteries, his back alive with fire. Sweat dribbled in beads between his shoulder blades. Nash winced. He cleared his throat, and his voice came thin: "I was convinced she would quit, go sell her story to some gossip rag. Or tell Carrol what she saw. I had no idea. But she didn't. When I finally saw the maid again, she didn't say a word, so I guess—*Ow!*"

"Maybe don't talk?"

"I don't think I'm ready for this. It's too much."

"We're in mid-process. Too late. Please, be still."

Nash shut his eyes so hard that hot tears wrung from his sockets. His hair felt drenched. His stomach flipped and his head filled with bees.

"There! Done." She took a full-length mirror from the wall and brought it him, giving him a good view of her work. He looked over his shoulder to see foot-long knitting needles piercing his skin in parallel columns. Tiny threads of blood leaked from openings.

My back... That's my back...

"No, you were right. I needed this," he said. "Hurts."

"Of course it does," Sara said, her grin wider than the grill of a car. "You've got twelve huge-ass knitting needles going through you."

"Take them out."

She began removing the needles and Nash gave his attention elsewhere to keep from passing out. On the wall in front of him was a framed poster advertising the movie "Rebel Without A Cause." Nash stared into James Dean's face, at his long, swept bangs like the swirls in a scoop of ice cream. Nash felt the last needle leave his flesh and he forgot about the poster, about Dean, about his comatose wife and dead daughter and about the police and the money and everything else but this insufferable, life-affirming pain.

Sara handed him a towel. "All better," she told him. "Let's go kill everyone."

19

There was a queen-sized bed, unmade, *Star Wars* comforter. Dirty clothes and towels lay about the hotel room like gunned-down bodies. Drexel's surfboard stood propped against the far wall, its tip against the corner. A dwarfish hotel manager, wearing comma-shaped bangs and a NO CASTRO NO PROBLEMA T-shirt, stood at the door and held it open. He shifted his feet and sighed continuously, not bothering to hide his agitation at having them in there.

Trace and Enrique had attained a search warrant for Drexel's hotel room, something which would have been done sooner were it not for the Miami-Dade County's erratic holiday hours. To complicate things further, the hotel manager spoke marginal English and, at first, wouldn't respect the warrant's relevance. Their badges and Enrique's Spanish were the exclusive reasons they'd gotten near the hotel room at all.

Inside, the two detectives searched for anything which might help strengthen the case even further. Neither Nash nor Drexel answered their phones and Ophelia wasn't cooperating. They didn't know what else to do. They looked for a letter mentioning what had happened, or for more illicit substances, or scribbled phone messages, or even Drexel himself maybe. No such luck.

Trace dug through a plastic wastebasket and uncrumpled each sheet of paper as he removed it...Doodlings (genitalia, circles and triangles, people with outlandish deformities) and phone numbers. He copied the numbers into his phone before placing them into a Ziploc evidence bag. After thinking about it, he dropped the doodlings in as well.

"*¿Cuando fue la utlima vez que lo vista?*" Enrique asked the hotel manager.

"*Hace una semana,*" the manager said. "*Tal vez.*"

Enrique translated for Trace: "He says he hasn't seen him in about a week." Enrique proceeded to shuffle through a dresser drawer, but there wasn't much there.

The majority of Drexel's wardrobe had been displaced about the room. He inventoried another dresser. "Bullshit, bullshit, more bullshit."

Trace kicked aside shirts and pants on the floor. After nudging aside a black tanktop, he found a small, vinyl-covered, spiral-bound book, the words ALLISON TAYLOR, INC. in rainbow script across the cover. It was a modeling portfolio book, belonging to "Ophelia Lake."

Her.

Trace picked up the book and tucked it inside his jacket before Enrique could see. "Find anything?" he asked him.

"Some pictures," Enrique said.

Trace walked over and stood beside him. He watched with Enrique as he peeled through an inch-thick block of photographs. The first dozen were of tattooed young people spotlighted by the camera's flash. They stood amongst a crowded gathering of some sort. They smiled and made faces and held drinks. There were several photographs of Drexel Waters himself with Ophelia, except with darker hair. In one photograph, she lay across his lap and stuck her tongue out at the camera.

Trace later spotted a birthday card beneath the bed. Garfield the Cat making a wisecrack about age. Inside the card was written:

"*Garfield's been throwing the coochy at me! Psyche!! What*

up, Drex? We got pretty lit last night, huh? Love them rum slushy-type concoctions. Want you to know that being with yo evil ass has made me the happiest chick in the whole wide universe. Happy B-Day! More presents later. I can only give them to you in PRIVATE (Whaaaaat?) Check me on the flipside. Love you infinitely A-ight? – Ophelia

Trace recalled seeing Ophelia as she'd arrived to meet him last night, the moment he saw her unfolding from a cab. The complications and worries of his current days could be temporarily set aside. And what sedated him was that over there – a collection of nerves and organs and blood so exquisitely packaged within a slim skeleton, wrapped by a smooth, bronze hide, cooked to medium-rare, the whole thing cooperating its way from a sit to a stand. And her walk, the way she put one foot in front of the other, like walking was a performance.

He imagined Ophelia with Drexel. Together. Taking walks. Sharing time. Being intimate. Trace had the vague urge to drop to his side, curl up, and weep. He also wanted to kick stuff until it broke and he imagined himself doing so.

"What is that?" Enrique asked from across the room. He'd been looking through what appeared to be Drexel's own portfolio book.

"What? This?"

"Yeah, that. In your hand. The card you're holding."

"It's nothing," he said. "I'm just...Don't worry about it. Are we done here?"

20

Big smile. Lean back. Okay. A little. A little more. Little more. There we go. Look at me. Keep your eyes on my nose. Little more. Move your hand. That's right. That's terrific. Other side. Good. All the way. Terrific. That's wonderful. Great. All right. Terrific. More of that. Very nice. Verrrrry nice. Love that. That's great. Looking great. Turn around now. Face me. Okay. Yes. Like that. Keep that up. Right there. Keep going. Wait. Go back some. Hold it for me. Hold it. Hold it. Right where you are. Hold still. Hold it. Now try and bend your knee a little. Little more. Uhp, too much. More to your left. Back, I mean. There. No. Over. Over. You got it. All right. Right there. Now don't breathe. Don't even breathe.

The Delano Hotel. Between shooting sessions, Ophelia used the hotel's basement bathroom to change outfits. Her fourth time in there, she heard the voices of two men through the door.

She heard their footsteps descending the stairs, coming in her direction. She'd locked the bathroom but had a premonition of the door opening for them anyway. She tested the knob

—locked. She grabbed it with both hands for further insurance. The voices and footsteps entered a room across the hall.

"Look, look," one of the voices said. "I'd eat her out like this...Look."

The other made a humored hiss. "Did you see the red thing she had on? With the thong thing? And when she leaned back? Did you witness? Makes you want to become a photographer, huh?"

"Ask me if I'd fuck her."

"Of course you would."

"But ask me."

"Would you fuck her?"

"Like this: Uh uh uh uh uh uh uh uh."

Their cackling echoed long and loud, like something heard in horror movies. They must have left their door open.

Moving with as much silence as possible, Ophelia finished wedging the cleavage pads into her chemise.

There was more laughter and a small sawing sound interspersed with ripping and knocking sounds...*Saw, rip, rip, saw, knock, rip, knock...*

Ophelia would have preferred spending eternity in the bathroom, or until the two men went away, whichever came first; but upstairs waited an entire fashion crew, including a photographer, his two assistants, hair stylist, make up stylist, clothing stylist, production coordinator, props person, production assistant, two male models, and some clean-cut man in a suit whose only purpose Ophelia could determine was to watch the shoot while talking on his phone. She'd been gone far too long as it was.

She waited for the men to leave, but whatever they were doing didn't sound too hurried. Their conversation didn't convey much haste either. No more waiting. She had to return to the site, the lobby. She had to. She put on her robe and counted to ten. To twenty.

Ophelia told herself not to look, but her eyes betrayed her. Though she only peeked, in instant, she saw the men were actually her own age. They stood in a kitchen of some sort, framed by pots hanging from hooks, suspended over a blood-splattered counter. The boys were separating beef ribs with butcher knives, their white smocks clouded pink. They turned at the sound of her door. Their mouths fell open.

Ophelia jogged up the stairs to the lobby, their horror movie-laughter pushing up from below.

His car was a pumpkin-colored 1977 Chevy Chevelle convertible, the coolest car she'd ever seen. A black circle with the white number "69" decorated the driver side door, a black and pink racing stripe on the other. It had been a twelve-hour day of shooting and the photographer was giving her a ride back to her hotel. They shared a joint and a bag of *Gummy Bears.* His name was Cool Dude Luv.

The shoot had been a disappointing experience. Puzzling even. He'd used her for all four of the most hackneyed pictures in fashion photography: 1. In a bikini, knee-deep in the ocean, splashing water at the camera. 2. Running in mid-spring. 3. On her back with her legs raised against a wall. 4. Standing by the side of the road, pretending to hitchhike. Perhaps he was making a statement.

While driving, Cool Dude Luv spoke without pause. She tried to pay attention, but he spoke so fast that her stoned mind drifted. She grew transfixed with his key chain, hanging from the ignition. The engine's clogged mutter caused the key chain to swing and vibrate while a pencil-thin bar of light, provided by the rearview mirror, allowed her alternating glimpses of the key chain's Elvis, his plump lips stretched into one of those *glory-glory-hallelujah* howls. He was sweaty and fat and dressed like Evel Knievel.

Cool Dude Luv reached into the *Gummy Bears* bag between them and came out with an orange one. "I am a widdle Gummy Bear," he sang-said while moving the bear back and forth in an arc. He bit the bear's head off.

Ophelia giggled. She took out a red one. She mimicked a high-pitched, helpless voice, a gurgling cry as it was swallowed. "Oh no, oh no, help me, help me...pleeeeaasse..."

"I can tell you like me," Cool Dude Luv said. "Would you like to have sex with me?"

"Do what?"

They came to a red light and Cool Dude Luv stopped his car. He turned in his seat to her. "Ophelia, you're an incredibly beautiful girl. One of the most stunning I've ever worked with. You could be famous. Like, Cindy Crawford famous. You're going to make a lot of people a lot of money, including yourself. And I'd like to help you do it."

She crossed her hands over her heart. "Are you serious?"

"You and I could accomplish a lot." After holding her eyes a while, he took her hand in his and placed it over his crotch. "But you have to make *me* happy first, you know?"

She tried to remove her hand, but he forced it back. "Wait, no, no, don't be scared. It's okay. S'kay! Hear me out before you freak. This'll be the smartest thing you've ever done. Go with it—Hey!" He gave her a short, hard shake. "It's not that big of a deal, all right? Think about the business you're in. You have to expect situations like this." He settled an arm around her. "Ophelia, chill. I'll help you out and I don't help just anybody. This is a big opportunity for you." He began kneading his crotch with her hand. The traffic light turned green. "Now all you have to do is make a pit stop with me at my penthouse. Do you understand why?"

Her face softened. She nodded.

"And we're cool? We're calm?"

She nodded again, smiled. She began some kneading of her own, cupping his balls softly.

"Great, I'll bet you're a real vacuum cleaner, aren't you? Hell yeah, you are." Cool Dude Luv smiled back. "This is going to be fun for you, too. Know why? Because you've never had someone like me. I'm the greatest lover alive. Ask any girl I've worked with. I'm going to blow your mind."

Though his erection couldn't get any stiffer, she massaged him with increasing encouragement.

"Feels great," he said. "How about taking a few puffs on my dick while I drive?"

"I would love that, yeah."

He let go of her to unzip himself.

She lunged for her door handle, but it slipped out of her hand. She tried again and the same. Again and the same. Like the stupid thing was greased. Cool Dude Luv reached across to stop her and pinned Ophelia against her door. This actually steadied her enough that her hands found the right grip on the handle. She rolled out of the car and onto her side.

"Stupid cunt!" he growled. He came partway out of the car after her.

Fuck this sleazy business! She was already thinking this as she fell to the ground. She was done. The end. She'd waited a safe amount of time. The timing of this was perfect actually.

Ophelia got to her feet, already winded, far too winded to run. She ran.

21

A Day-Glo mural of red and yellow skeletons copulating jubilantly wrapped the interior of Dante's Nightclub. Dark-clothed people converged at the bar as though it were a fire and the club were freezing. A mushroom-haired barmaid cradled a phone between her neck and shoulder, fingers *busybusybusy* with a computer-screened register, coating her in a blue and oily haze.

"Is it loud in here or what?" Enrique shouted, thereby, answering his own question.

Trace plugged his ears. "Ridiculous!"

They shared a look around them. "See her anywhere?" Enrique asked. "What time did she say she'd be here?"

"Around about now."

"So she said she'll do it now? You believe her?"

"One way to find out."

"This is such great news!"

"You sure about this? What we're doing?"

"Stop asking that! Let's check the bar!"

Trace traced the half-filled dance floor. Enrique followed with his hands in his pockets, arms locked straight, seemingly horrified at the thought of anyone touching him. They were here because Ophelia had texted Trace. Her message claimed she was ready to go through with it. She would tape Drexel.

Behind the bar, a rectangular funhouse mirror wobbled along the wall. As Trace and Enrique approached, their deformed reflections elasticized from out of a small, pink orb. Trace's stomach ballooned while the rest of him dwindled. Enrique's gigantic head appeared to have been mashed flat by a gigantic mallet. Around them, the seated patrons created a fleshy smear punctured with eyes and mouths. Tacked along the bar's wooden frame, cluttered like fish scales, hung Polaroids of attractive, well-dressed people holding drinks, all of them popeyed and senseless from the camera's flash.

A minute on the phone and the barmaid hung up. She took a rag from off her shoulder and began wiping the bar. She made brief eye contact with them but continued wiping.

"Hi!" Trace megaphoned with his hand. "Hello! Excuse me! Hey!"

She lifted her brows at him.

"Do you know Ophelia Lake?"

She leaned towards him. "Who?"

"Ophelia Lake! Do you know her?"

He offered his ear at her and she bellowed at it. "I've seen her here before! Not tonight though!"

Trace brought his wallet out from its place in his coat pocket. He blossomed the wallet at her, showing the badge, then he introduced himself. He waited for Enrique to do the same, but he was looking around them, too preoccupied with the loud, colorful commotion of the club.

"We're going to have a seat and wait a while!" Trace shouted to her. "You mind?"

"Sure, whatever!" She flipped two wafer-thin cork coasters onto the bar before them. "Something to drink?"

Trace nudged Enrique. "Something to drink?"

"Me? No! Are you drinking?"

"Bloody Mary!" Trace shouted at her. "Light on the blood, thank you!"

She leaned forward again and squinted, not hearing him.

"Bloody Mary! Light on the blood! Please!"

The bartender nodded. She snatched glasses from here and there, poured this and that liquid together. She shook them into fusion.

Trace had to nudge Enrique from looking round again. "Let me call her."

"What?"

Trace took out his phone and instead texted Ophelia that they were there. Where was she? Trace ingested half his Bloody Mary in the first downing. He coughed.

"Why are you drinking?" Enrique asked him. "Nervous?"

"A little, yeah. This isn't easy." Another gulp and Trace had killed the near-Bloodless Mary. He touched his glass to his forehead.

Electronic drumbeats tested the building's foundation, the sole lyrics being that of a woman screaming. And screaming. The combination sawed at every branch in Trace's nervous system, at the same time, serving as a soundtrack to silhouetted people dancing within fat smoke banks. Crisp cones of colored light twirled and flashed about them in dramatic ray-gun duels.

Trace raised his drink at Enrique. "I'm getting drunk! Sure you don't want just one drink?"

Enrique's smirk carved open his left cheek. "You're not falling apart on me, are you?"

Trace looked into the bottom of his glass and swirled the melted ice around. He drank the ice. "I'm good."

"I was beginning to think you were tipping this guy off."

"That's a hell of a thing to accuse me of, partner."

"I'm just saying. If it was one of *my* good buddies…"

"I'm walking a fine line here, okay? I'm coming down on a friend. It's not easy."

"Does he have anything to do with what happened to your face?"

"Told you already. Just some asshole." Trace took a small digital voice recorder from his inside jacket pocket. "This should do the job. It's got built-in memory, so it will practically record forever. High quality audio. Battery's aren't new but should be fine."

"I'm going to go look around for her."

"How do you know what she looks like?"

"She's a model, right? I'll look for a girl who's ten feet tall and weighs about that many pounds. If it's not her, I'm sure she'll know her."

Trace watched him leave. He went back to the bar.

When the bartender fluttered past, holding dollar bills to feed the register with, Trace waved for her attention. Though there were several other customers already doing the same, Trace won her attention first. She aimed her ear at him. One of the perks in having the power to arrest people was that you were seldom inconvenienced. He asked for *Southern Comfort* on the Rocks.

His next question inquiring her name was left hanging. She hadn't heard him.

Half-hour later, the people populating the bar multiplied into a noisy pile of faces and arms. Trace glanced at the admission stamp on the back of his hand: a fuzzy, blue hourglass. The same song which had been playing when he and Enrique entered started up again. Or perhaps it never ended.

Enrique appeared next to him, hatched from an iridescent membrane of dancers. "Couldn't find her."

"I don't know what to tell you!"

"I can't take another second of this place! I'm getting claustrophobic!"

Trace became rocked by a sudden, soggy feeling of futility and emptiness. He reached inside his jacket and came back out with his wallet. He unpinned the badge from inside and handed it to him. "Flush this for me, will you?"

Enrique's struggle to suppress his shock was truly something to behold. He looked at Trace's badge in his hand. He bounced his hand as if testing the badge's weight. "Okay, you're shit-faced, right?" Enrique looked up at him. "It's why you're acting this way! Talking shit! Tomorrow you'll wake up with a hangover, take some aspirin, drink some coffee, and we'll move forward! Everything's going to be hunky-dory! Agreed?"

He raised Trace's hand by the wrist and slapped the badge into it.

Trace worked his tongue around in his mouth, putting the badge away. He took a tissue from another pocket and used it for his nose. "I'm sick," he said.

"Okay! So! *Mañana* then!" Enrique excused himself repeatedly while prying a path towards the front entrance.

"Look! I hate this! That you've become the way you are!" Trace shouted at Enrique's back, his last word cut short by a cough. "I wish there was something I could do!"

He finished coughing into his fist. He cleared his throat and loosened his tie. Damn thing was tight as a noose.

22

Ophelia closed her eyes and through the veil of her lids, she saw blue, yellow, red, purple, white, green, red, blue, yellow. There was nothing like dancing on cocaine. Shut your brain off and let your heart dictate the movement, the tympanic beat matching it pulse for pulse. Let your hair drop over your face and hide yourself, only you and the music and your heart and the colored lights coming through your lids and it was all you needed.

She tried pretending the dance floor wasn't as jammed as it was, but when someone stepped on her foot, it reminded her why she never came to Dante's anymore. Place was getting too popular.

She knew Drexel was already here himself somewhere. She could feel him. Besides, he adored the whole "Divine Comedy" concept, the club's three floors representing The Inferno, Purgatory, and Paradise in ascending order. It was the coolest to him, the coolest to everyone. The club had been open for five years, and, in South Beach time, this was equivalent to centuries.

Paradise consisted of white walls with hills of foam pumped onto the dance floor, transvestite dancers in angelic costuming. Purgatory was bathrooms with a chubby-cushioned hangout area and coat check. Inferno: black walls and a black floor spinning within a galaxy of tiny luminescent circles, the result of a disco ball's spherically-split light. Two glass-topped bars bordered the room, lit from within by a seeping red glow, which also lit the ceiling.

Inferno was where Ophelia danced.

As she left the dance floor, she was yanked to the right. When she saw that it was Drexel who had her arm, she cried out and flinched. She tried to raise her arms over her head, but he held the left one down and forced something onto her pinkie.

Ophelia straightened herself, embarrassed by her reaction. She brought the pinkie towards her face. "What is this?" she asked, though she could clearly see that it was a ring.

"It's for you," Drexel said.

The ring was almost diminutive; it wouldn't fit any lower than her knuckle. A toy ring, the band chipped and scratched. It was crowned by a fake, red emerald the size of a cough drop. Encased inside, a picture of a butterfly...a butterfly? She looked closer. "What is it? A chicken?"

Drexel nodded, overjoyed with himself, and was bumped. They were both nudged from one stance to another by the people in movement around them.

She tossed her head back to get her bangs out of her eyes. "Gee, you must've paid a fortune."

"Not a cent. I stole it from this old homeless lady in a wheelchair. I snuck up behind her and...*Bam!*" He made the motion of bashing someone's face in with his elbow. "And I ran away. All for you."

"You wouldn't hurt an old lady."

"Anything for you."

"Right." She stretched her arm out and moved her hand around. "Where have you been?"

"Missing you like crazy. Can you get me some coke?"

"What do I look like, your dealer?"

He stepped towards her. She backed up.

"What?" Drexel seemed genuinely surprised. "I was going to kiss you."

"Do not touch me. As in, ever again." On cue, she was bumped from behind by someone dancing.

"What do you want me to do? Get on my hands and knees and grovel? I'll do it. Name it."

"How could you talk to me like that, Drexel? A guy doesn't say those kinds of things to his girlfriend! And, my God, some girl is dead because of you!"

"I told you I was sorry, didn't I?"

"Oh, gosh, well, that makes everything instantly better."

"Good." He went to kiss her again. She moved. "Ophelia!"

"No, let's see you grovel. Like you said. I want it."

Drexel scraped the ceiling with his gaze, plowed his hands in his pockets. A strobe light fluttered staccato light over him. He said, "I'm leaving this city. I'm going away. I want you to come with me."

"I don't want to go to jail, Drexel."

"I'll say I kidnapped you."

"I'll bet if I threw holy water on you, it would burn."

"Is that a yes?"

"Where would we even go, Drexel?"

"Anywhere but here. Find us some coke and we can talk about it."

"Do you have money?"

"Not much."

"Won't you need some for your great escape?"

"You'll figure something out, won't you? Don't you always?"

Ophelia didn't check her purse for the scrap of paper until she reached Purgatory. There, a disordered search came up empty. Must have left the dealer's number at the hotel or at Drexel's or where?

"You're a fucking liar," said the girl in overalls and black combat boots, her head shaved except for a fringe of blue bangs.

She spoke into her phone while standing near Ophelia. "You're not going to get away with lying to me," the girl said.

Amassed in Purgatory were other people on other phones, a long line at the girl's restroom, plump cushions with people in them. A few of the people made out, others smoked and talked, some sat and stared, because there was nothing else to do, who knew, because they were thinking. A fogbank of cigar and cigarette smoke made the other side of the room appear far more than distant than it was.

She called her dealer, but he was dry. Or, more likely, not motivated by the asking amount. He gave her another number to try, but she wasn't sure she'd heard it right. She asked him to repeat it, but he'd hung up. Ophelia texted him to ask for the number again but realized he would never do it.

Ophelia stared at the tic-tac-toe of dial numbers on her phone's touch screen. She tried rearranging them into the ones she needed. 673...16 – 672? Wait. 6? 7? 671? 673?

"You are a fuck-ing liar," the shaved-headed girl barked into her phone. "How dare you destroy every day of my life? You're a liar. No, you're a liar."

As best as she could, Ophelia pieced together the phone number. She dialed.

"See? You're a liar...Because you're a liar, that's why. Why do you want to lie to me?"

An elderly woman wheezed hello and Ophelia hung up. Totally the wrong number.

"Don't lie to me! You're such a liar! No, I'm not okay!"

Ophelia meditated, trying for a final time to conjure the dealer's phone number. She tried for another number combination that felt somewhat familiar. A man answered.

"Darby?"

"Who?"

"Is this Darby?"

"Darby?"

"Is Darby there?"

"Who is this?"

"I must have the wrong number. Sorry."

"Ophelia?"

She went to end the call, but stopped herself, having caught the meaning of what she'd heard. She brought the phone back to her ear. "Hello?"

"Sweetheart?"

The voice. It still took her a moment. "Daddy?"

"Where are you, hon?" he asked her.

The truth was too heavy but it came out anyway. "In a nightclub," she said.

"In Miami?"

"In South Beach, yeah."

"Gracious! Sounds like you're in a machine shop. It's, ah, it's almost midnight, honey."

"Is it? Oh."

"Why are you calling? Everything okay?"

"Um, yeah. I didn't know it was so late though. I'll let you get back to sleep."

"Sweetie, are you okay? Why are you calling?"

"I didn't mean to."

"You sure? There's nothing you want to tell me?"

"No, I was trying to call someone else. Go back to sleep."

"I'm here for you, hon. Please, tell me if something's wrong. I want to know. You don't sound...right."

"I'm fine. I'm great."

"Your mother tells me you're dating some Spanish fellow?"

She ended the call. She kept her phone cupped in both hands as she lay her forehead against her wrists. She swallowed hard. Ophelia raised her head, texted Trace. She apologized and told him she'd gotten held up. Everything was back on track.

"Because you're a liar, you're nothing but a liar," continued the shaved-headed girl. "That's why."

23

Riding over The MacArthur Causeway in a taxi, Gary Nash noticed the Port of Miami to his right, the cruise ships parked there like shiny, smooth icebergs. Sara sat pensive beside him, thumbnail moon through her window. Nash decided to check his voicemail.

First message was from Detective Trace Strickland, only checking in. Still no definite progress, but he'd be sure to let Nash know. Second message was from his sister Caroline sounding concerned and nervous as always, even back when there was never a reason to be. Third message was from the Executive Vice President of Business Operations with The New York Mets, inviting Nash to be a luncheon speaker at The New York State Foundation of Accounting Education's Real Estate Conference.

Who was this jackoff? Didn't he know what Nash was going through? Didn't he read the goddamn newspaper? Did anyone?

The fourth and fifth messages were hang-ups. Nothing about an unconscious paparazzo in his wife's hospital room. Not a word. Not yet. That *did* happen, right?

He took the .32 from inside the front of his pants, keeping it low to avoid the taxi driver's line of sight. He checked the safety for the hundredth time before placing it back inside his pants. The Wave Hotel. He'd made a point to remember the name. Such an obvious, uncreative name. He hated the hotel already. The taxi driver assured Nash that he knew exactly where to take them: Ocean and Fourth.

Nash's back stuck to the seat, so he stayed sitting forward. The places where the needles had pierced his flesh buzzed, stinging, still damp from leaky band-aids.

"You okay?" Sara touched his shoulder.

He winced. "No. You?"

"You give me as much money as you're promising, Gary, and everything is okay with me forever."

"Delighted you think so." He thought of Carol and what had happened to her. He struggled to control his emotions. No, there would be time for deep sorrow later.

He looked curiously at the back of the taxi driver's neck, a heavily creased patch of hairy skin with several papilloma marks. Nash considered what forms and levels of suffering inflicted this man's life. There had to be conflict. Perhaps this was why someone would call him at a time like this about some stupid conference. Living could be overwhelming. You lose track. Maybe this guy's wife was sleeping with his best friend. A gambling problem prevented him from affording his mortgage. Maybe the taxi driver had a brother with cancer and a father who didn't care. Everyone had battles. Maybe Drexel didn't deserve to die. He could have genuinely loved Holly and be devastated from her death, same as him.

Then why didn't he help her? What kind of monster?

Nash carefully slid the gun back into his pocket. He wiped his eyes, took out his phone again. He called Trace back. No answer. Just as well. Nothing was stopping him now anyway.

24

Someone was puking in the nightclub's bathroom. Five of what Trace assumed were the poor guy's friends crowded the open stall. For a better view, a pair of them stood atop the commodes on either side. Together, the friends chanted: "Go, Bobby, go! Go, Bobby, go! Go, Bobby, go!"

Trace washed his face in the sink, wondering what exactly he should do next. He had entered the bathroom to call Ophelia. She'd texted him that she was there finally. Got held up. However, the noise of the guys chanting at their sick friend made calling her impossible. The dance music was too loud through the walls anyway. He texted her to meet him by the stairs.

He cupped water and ran it over his hair. The water dripped from his nose and chin as he began a staring contest with the mirror. A forty-watt bulb above the mirror spilled triangular shadows below his eyes, shadows which vanished beyond his jaw. A cut on his bottom lip was scabbing, developing a greenish tumescence. The swelling beneath his left eye had gone from blue to lavender. He looked terrible. Hideous. Looking like this, how could he hope to keep the interest of a girl like Ophelia anyway? Let her go to Drexel. Let them get married while he's in jail and live miserably ever after. Wasn't Trace's concern anymore. He only cared about his share of the money now. Saving Casey.

He turned at the sound of Bobby emerging from his stall. His face held the slack, bloodless expression that faces normally hold after their mouths have reversed their purpose. Bobby's friends patted his shoulders and ruffled his hair in a congratulatory way. It was obvious they loved him, didn't matter how much of a mess he made. Never would. They were his friends.

Ascending the stairs to Purgatory, the walls playing Ping-Pong with him, Trace felt as though he were either exiting or entering a birth canal. The walls were womb-tinted. Neon ran up both walls in bright, squiggly lines.

Someone touched his arm as a shirtless man—muscles big enough that they disallowed his arms from touching his sides—passed between them, going up the stairs.

"There you are." It was Ophelia.

"Here I am." Trace coughed, leaned his back against the stairway wall, next to a corkboard feathered with flyers. The two of them stood lathered in pink light.

"How do we do this?" she asked him. "Do I put a wire on beneath my clothes?"

"This is all you need." He removed the digital mini-recorder from his jacket and handed it to her. "It's nothing too sophisticated. Keep it in your purse."

"Why can't I just use my phone?"

Trace went to respond but had to wait as a sequined shirt and sharkskin pants passed between them, descending the stairs. "It's better this way. Too many footprints for you. Trust me."

Leopard print tights and a china-doll haircut passed between them, descending. Next, a denim tube dress with red fishnets, descending.

"If Drexel goes to jail, I don't know what I'll do." Ophelia leaned her shoulder against the wall, then her head. "Have you ever wished you could get a fake death certificate with your name on it and start your life over as someone completely different?"

"People have tried it."

Ophelia studied the mini-recorder in her hands. She put the recorder in her purse and circulated her hand through its guts. She came out with a small, dark vial and held it to the light before tapping the vial's bottom. She took out a glob of keys, separating the biggest key from the rest and inserting it into the vial. She brought the key below her nose and snorted cocaine from the end of it.

"Have some," she said. "It'll make your face feel better."

Trace accepted the key and the vial from her. He scrapped out a small bump. He pushed one nostril shut, used the other nostril to inhale. "Look at me," he said, sniffling. "You make me insane."

She took the key and the vial back. "He's here, you know."

"Derxel?"

"He's upstairs." Ophelia snorted two more times, giving them to the same nostril. She pinched her nostrils together. "*Owww, ma nodes errts.*"

"You're huffing that stuff up like it was oxygen. Slow down."

Ophelia fanned herself as her face wilted, lines forming on her forehead, mouth opening, turning down, sneeze coming, coming, coming...She achooed blood. It spattered her hands, the lower part of her face. "Ah! *Gah*..."

"Holy shit!" He touched her shoulder.

She sneezed once more, blood-free this time. She searched frantically within her purse. "Dammit, I don't have a tissue."

"You okay?"

"I need something to wipe my face with."

He ripped a flyer from the corkboard and handed it to her. But the paper wasn't absorbent enough. The blood only smeared.

"Wait for me here while I go into the bathroom," she said. "Dammit, people are looking at me."

"Here. Use my shirt."

"But it's white."

He removed his blazer and the T-shirt. He handed her the T-shirt and she thanked him.

"Mind if I ask you a question?" he asked her while putting his blazer back on. "What exactly do you see in him?"

"Who? Drexel?" She finished wiping her face and her hands. It took a while.

He almost thought she'd forgotten the question before realizing that maybe this wasn't the most appropriate time to be asking. Rattled by her gruesome sneeze, the question had simply lept out of him, sprung from fright, having rested on the tip of his tongue ever since meeting her.

At last she said, "He's the only boyfriend I've ever had who's never told me I was pretty."

"No, I asked you what you *saw* in him. I meant, the *good* stuff which keeps you with him."

"I understood what you meant. He's never told me I was pretty and that's a *good* thing. Means he sees something in me that no one else does, something more than my looks."

"Ophelia, look at me."

She was already looking at him.

"You're one of the prettiest girls I have ever laid eyes on," Trace said. "It's true. You're so incredibly beautiful."

She rolled her eyes and it appeared she might start laughing until her face changed. Her bottom lip quivered. She broke the stare before the moistness in her eyes could spill over. She cleared her throat. "Thank you," she said, barely audible. Ophelia sighed. She held his bloody shirt out by its shoulders. "Yuck. Blood. It's everywhere lately."

He moved over to stand beside her. "It's like one of those ink tests psychiatrists give people." He pointed at the drying blood. "Look, there's the sun."

"Where? Oh! Or it's a planet exploding."

"See the smiley face?"

"A smiley face? No way. Wait, there it is. A smiley face. Check that out. A bloody smiley face...I did something good."

"I should warn you I'm probably falling in love with you."

She remained holding the shirt. She turned her head to him. "I was hoping you would say that actually."

Trace felt his heart inside his tonsils. He was trying not to smile but knew that the joy on his face was evident there anyway. *She was hoping he would say that?* "What's your plan?" he asked her.

"I'll go back to Drexel now. I'll get him to leave and talk and I'll tape it. As much as I can. That's what you want, right?"

"Specifically get him to talk about what happened that night in the hotel room. At the party. As much detail as possible."

Ophelia lowered her arms. She lowered her head until it touched Trace's shoulder. "Then come get me? Take me somewhere else?"

He closed his arms around her. He agreed to do whatever she wanted.

25

N ash stood with Sara across the street from The Wave, a four-story, art deco hotel, sitting quiet and dark. He had to act fast. Sky was getting brighter by the second. Still not many people around, but that would soon change. Small bugs zipped around them in loopy circles, straying from an insect flight jam between street lamps.

Nash handed her the gun, waited for her to turn it on him. She didn't.

"How do I fire it?" she asked. "Just point it and shoot, right?"

"You've never fired a gun?"

"Seen people do it on TV. Looks easy."

He back-stepped and turned away. Too late now. This was the best assassin at-hand. While working in the scumbag world of luxury New York real estate, he'd never managed to meet any hitmen or mob guys. He knew people who likely employed them, but too many of these same people would turn Nash over in a heartbeat. Seeing him go down for a crime so scandalous would be a Disney dream come true. This was the only way.

Nash decided to use some of his real estate acumen to tactically reviewed the hotel's design and landscape, analyze advantages. He calculated Sara climbing the tallest palm tree nearest the southeast wall. She could possibly crawl onto the deco eyebrow which ran beneath the hotel's front windows.

However, she could also get sliced up from the sharp leaves and pointy bark. If needing the extra help to climb, she could try digging her fingers into the inverted speed lines of the building. From what Nash recalled from an Architecture class at Columbia, these art deco features were meant to emphasize the horizontal qualities of the hotel, allowing stresses to stream away from the building's edge. Also helpful for climbing though. Hopefully.

After a brief fit of pacing, Nash decided he would get Sara to at least *attempt* the climb. She could scoot along and search the open windows. She would have to find a way in. She just would.

Another taxi pulled to the front. It sat there for some minutes before a tall couple got out. Nash saw Drexel's profile and recognized him right away. He'd seen that profile many times online during feverish, late-night research. He'd even saved a picture of the loser in his phone.

Nash watched Drexel and a blonde girl trot the front patio steps. Was this "the girlfriend" the detectives had mentioned? Nash had nearly forgotten about their arrangement. Only agreed for the sake of keeping the detectives busy and off his back while he figured out what he actually wanted to do.

He watched as Drexel tried opening the hotel's glass front door, but it was locked. He rapped the glass and was soon let in by someone in a hotel uniform—a long, gray coat laced in red and gold, like that of a Confederate soldier.

Sara noticed Nash's alertness while watching them. "It's him?" she whispered. "It is, isn't it?"

A few minutes later, a light came on in one of the second story windows, from a room facing the street. This was turning out to be too easy.

Architecture.

26

Inside the hotel, Drexel and Ophelia took a shower together and Drexel picked this moment, of all moments, to decide he was horny. Ophelia resisted at first but not much. She gave in, thinking, *"Sure, why not. Let's do it."* Forget their problems, forget everything, go at it like animals. Over the edge and beyond. Yippee. She held the wash rack for balance. She worried about them being taped from the mini-recorder, though she doubted any of this could get picked up from her purse, all the way from its place on the bed. Or maybe the recorder was picking up every single noise. She didn't care. The recorder had been on for two hours already, but Drexel had been uncharacteristically quiet while riding back.

A few minutes into making love, Ophelia began laughing.

"What's funny?" Drexel asked. He stopped.

She covered her mouth with her hand. "Nothing," she said. "Don't stop."

He continued and for a while everything was as it had been, only the sound of the shower, the heavy slapping of his thighs against her ass. The sounds of their sex grew louder, and Ophelia lost it again, truly guffawing this time. Her laughter echoed off the too-close tiled walls.

Drexel went to his knees. He pressed his face into her ass, licking at her until she stopped laughing. He sat back and carefully eased a finger inside the puffy button of her asshole. He worked the finger in as far as he could while another two fingers massaged her clit beneath. Ophelia buckled, wincing.

He soon slipped into having a seat, as if his knees could no longer support him, not for one second more. The shower's spray ricocheted off the top of his head. He wiped water from his eyes. It gushed down his face and body.

"You all right?" Ophelia sat in front of him, meditation-style, same as him. There wasn't enough room to sit any other way. The water poured over them.

"It's been a while since I slept," he said. "Plus, those shrooms. I'm exhausted."

"You took mushrooms?"

Steam accumulated between them so that he became blurred to her, as though seeing him through gauze. The steam made the air thick, harder to breathe.

"Probably I should kill myself," he said. "I tried once. I ever tell you before?"

She looked at the phrase "kill myself" in front of her and recoiled from it. "Don't talk shit, okay?"

"Took a whole bottle of aspirin. Man, I despised myself. Everybody did. I was the most hated kid in school. My family even hated me. Daddy the most."

The water, she could swear, was growing hotter. She lay her hand on the side of his neck. "Let's get out of the shower, huh?"

"No matter who you become or what you accomplish, your daddy will always be the one man above you. But as a kid, imagine, I was disgusting to look at. Pimples, braces, breasts. Girls used to touch me, then touch each other, and say, 'Ooooh, he's on you!' Imagine having a boy like that for your son? It would've pissed *me* off." It was Drexel's turn to laugh. When his laughter finished, the bathroom felt incredibly still. Ophelia glanced through the shower's sliding glass door and expected to see something move out there. But nothing moved.

"It's one reason why I've always felt such a connection

with you," he said. "You went through the same thing, sort of."

She swiped hair from her face. "I could never even picture you fat."

"Junior high. The only time of my life that was worse than prison."

"You won't kill yourself and you know it."

"I was thinking. We can hide out here till they find us and in the meantime we can get high and fuck, fuck and get high, then getting high and fucking and when they break down the door—" He bore his eyes into hers. "Well, I have the knife."

As she spoke, slowly, evenly, Ophelia imagined her words as letters on a string which she unspooled from her throat: "I am not supportive of that."

His expression didn't change. After a few minutes, he shook his head. "We need to go far away. If I'm going to break my parole, I'd better make sure I break it good. Anywhere outside Florida would be ideal."

She put her other hand against the other side of his neck. She raised to her knees and kissed him. "Shouldn't we be going? A while ago you didn't even want to come back here. Come on. Stand up."

"There is a third option," he said, rising with her help. "You could go to your Dad's and I could go to Mexico or to Puerto Rico. Until things died down. I'd come back for you."

"No, you wouldn't."

"Yes, I would."

"No, Drexel, no. I'd never see you again."

Drexel nodded, but slow and without looking at her. It seemed he'd heard her, though from a great distance, her voice a whisper from the other end of a long tunnel.

She slid the shower door open. Steam hurried out. The entire bathroom filled with a thick mist. The bathroom mirror turned from blurry to white. "Drexel, what are we doing?" she asked in a low voice. "We're screwed, aren't we? We might as well face it."

He kneeled, wrapped his arms around her legs, and

mashed his face into her thigh, hard enough that he had to breathe through his mouth. "One more time then? In case it's the last time?" He leaned back and looked up at her. "How about it? Spread yourself for me?"

She scooped up two handfuls of his hair and let it go. The hair spilled clumsily, thick with water. Ophelia turned around and bent over. Drexel grabbed her ass cheeks and squeezed them, running his hands over their fleshy tightness. He spread her ass apart and buried his face there. She reached over to shut the shower off, kill the distraction. The shower stream perished with a final jolt of freezing water, causing them both to yipe and jerk back.

Ophelia squatted above her jewelry box, the one she'd thrown at him two nights ago. She grabbed up chunks of knotted necklaces and replaced them in the box. She removed the chicken ring from her pinkie and put this inside also. She set the box in her opened, hard-backed suitcase, which lay open on her bed. Ophelia put on an orange sundress with heels and packed in the dark room.

"What are you bringing?" she asked him.

When she turned to see why he hadn't answered her, she saw that he lay on his back on the bed, out cold, snoring softly for once. She texted Trace that it was time. Come get me.

She started to leave, then realized she was forgetting her bathroom stuff. Towels and toiletries and such. First things first though. She went into the bathroom, got her vial out, and tapped out four lines onto the commode lid. She used a dollar bill for snorting, two lines for each nostril. She stood, sniffled, wiped her nose. She put the vial away in her purse, placed the purse on the floor.

She opened the cabinet beneath the sink. From there, she removed a hairbrush, *Tampax* box, a make-up pouch, a few perfume bottles, lotion, nail polish, and polish remover. She set the items on the commode lid. She opened the medicine cabinet, took toothpaste and toothbrush, handmirror, more make-up, more perfume, hair clips, and hair ties.

After she closed the cabinet, she caught a snap-second glimpse of her reflection in its mirror. The shadow beneath her nose was too long. She looked again. It wasn't a shadow.

"Ah, no, dammit!" she said. She tried putting a finger below her nose to stop the blood, but it kept coming. She dropped her arm and watched the mirror, shell-shocked as her reflection's nose proceeded to leak red lines which descended past her lips and chin. Her mouth fell open and she saw her teeth were bloody. The nosebleed had even dropped into her throat.

She backed away from the sink, her heart hammering. This was bad. She'd gotten nosebleeds before, sure, same as anyone. But this...blood was oozing out of her head! Ophelia wiped her face clean with a washcloth, then tried wringing the blood out. No use. Ruined. She ripped off a sheet of toilet paper, halved it, wadded the halves into balls. She used the balls to plug her nose. This made her look ridiculous but stopped the bleeding at least.

She took the blood-clotted tissues out of her nose and tossed them into the wastebasket. She tilted her head back to get a look inside. All clean, even on the sides. She left the bathroom with an armful of dirty clothes and dropped them inside her suitcase, replacing what fell out. Before closing the suitcase, she noticed her toothbrush. A quick brush wouldn't hurt. She'd swallowed most of the blood in her mouth, but it left a taste like coins. Another line or two wouldn't be a terrible idea either.

She re-entered the bathroom and approached the sink and froze. A small, sharp gasp escaped her. Something had somehow gone completely wrong with her reflection. *Had* to be wrong!

"OhmyGod, OhmyGod, no, no, no, stop, stop, oh shit." Two more trail lines of blood had left her nose, the right trail rounding the curvature of her lips. She touched the blood and it came off on her fingers. She folded her hands over the lower half of her face and leaned forward, almost touching eyeballs with her reflection.

Her hands shook. She began shaking all over, right down to her eyelids. Not wanting to drop her hands, she did anyway after noticing the sides of her palms were red.

She uncovered her face and nearly screamed. Her mouth opened to do so, but she stopped herself. Afraid she might never stop. She kept shaking, like she was freezing, yet sweated feverishly. The lower half of her face had become one large, dark-red blotch.

She covered her face again. "Oh, no, oh, God, oh, please, stop, please, stop, pleeeeeeease...shit, shit, shit...stop!"

Ophelia took her hands away. The blotch had spread to the upper part of her neck. More blood kept coming. She cried, soundless at first, then with long, raspy inhalations, which built into sobs.

She lifted the bath towel from the floor and used it on her face, bloodying the cloth, now also ruined.

She left the bathroom, crossed the room, opened its door, walked out. She went down the hallway. This was the way it had to happen if it would ever happen at all; or perhaps because seeing your own face slick with blood had a way of clarifying things. Having heard her father's voice on the phone tonight had also jarred something loose in her, some inner lid which had been sealed shut for far too long. Also, Drexel's talk of suicide. All this blood.

Ophelia took the stairs to the lobby.

27

Nash stood with Sara again, same spot across the street. It drizzled.

"See the ledge?" he asked her. He pointed at the hotel. "You're going to have to climb up there. Without the high-heels obviously."

"Shouldn't you be hiding somewhere? Let me do this."

"I already told you. We're in this together."

She rolled her eyes. "You can't control everything, Gary," she said.

"I've got it figured out how you're going to get into his room. I need you to listen."

"You're exactly like my youngest."

"See the window with the light on, right? Second floor?"

"Yes, I saw it. I was standing right here. I'll handle it. You need to leave."

"Wait, did you just say 'youngest?'"

A tumble of thunder sent the car alarm of a nearby Maserati into a momentary frenzy. WOWA! WOWA! WOWA! BAMP! BAMP! BAMP! BAMP! WHOOOOP! WHOOOOOP! WHOOO-OOOP! The outraged automobile sat parked in the hotel's shadow. It whistled, then went quiet.

"I have two daughters, yeah," Sara said. "Why else would I be doing this? I would do anything for them."

"You never told me you had kids."

"Yes, I have. You just don't remember. I'm not important to you." She regarded the rain clouds above them, then held her arms out, as if controlling the storm, conducting it. The Weather Witch. Beyond her, the beach appeared as a fuzzy glow through drapes of distant rain.

"I can't let you do this," Nash heard himself say. "Give me the gun back."

"It's too late. You've already transferred half the money to me."

"Keep it. I'll even send the rest when I'm done."

"Done with what? You're going to climb *your* old ass up there?"

"Sara, take off, all right? And never tell anyone you knew anything about any of this, okay?"

"I told you I had kids." She stepped closer to him. "I told you."

"Both of them girls?"

She nodded slow. The spaghetti straps of her tank-top rode her bony shoulders as if she were the loneliest woman alive.

Nash reached into his wallet and removed the cash from there. He handed it to her, folded in half. He slowly took back the .32 from her at the same time. "There," he said. "That's better."

She looked at the money in her hands. She looked at the gun. "I hope this brings you the peace you're looking for."

"It will." He spotted the black Lincoln over her shoulder, seeing the vehicle move for the first time. It rolled to a stop about a block away, across the street.

She went to touch him. "I hope—"

Nash raised the gun into the air and fired. The weapon's recoil and surprising boom nearly made him drop it. He didn't watch the people, but he was aware of some nearby crying out and running away.

One of them was Sara, her heels clicking down the sidewalk, a sound like a typewriter. He waited until the tap-tap-tap faded away before crossing the street towards the hotel.

Balanced along the narrow ledge, Gary Nash stopped crawling. He'd come across the room with the light on. He raised himself, keeping his back against the hotel's outer wall. He peeked through the window again, but kept his knees cocked, ready to spring back if spotted.

The room's sole light source was a lamp by the window. A shape stirred from the bed. He took the gun from the back of his pants, where its barrel had nuzzled between his ass cheeks while he climbed. The window was drawn with blinders, but he could see in through a slat. No matter how hard Nash squinted though, he couldn't get a good look. Wanted to be extra sure. He needed to see the face. He pulled up on the window and it opened.

The traffic light went from yellow to pink. It didn't occur to Trace what this might signify, so he kept driving through the light. Drove fine, as a matter of fact. Perception clear as crystal. All he had to do was focus. Focus, focus. Simply had to remember he was drunk and wasn't supposed to be driving. He had to pay attention or else. He tried using a little of the Buddha stuff again, help keep steady. Or was it Zen?

Cassie, bless her heart, had regurgitated so many different philosophies at him, he could never keep up with which belief belonged to who. And what good had any of that crap done for her anyway?

He did recall her horoscope the day her life nearly ended. It predicted she was on the threshold of a long and solitary journey. He remembered this info since it'd been her habit to read her internet horoscope aloud from her phone. Also, it was because he shared the same horoscope. They were Geminis. Other than being extremists, he couldn't swear to what else "Gemini" supposedly described. Couldn't even recall what the damn mascot was. A man with a horse's body and a chicken's head holding a bucket of fish. Or a rifle. Maybe a raygun.

Where was that girl going? She walked down the sidewalk, staring at the ground, her face covered in paint. Or was it *blood*? He could've sworn the girl was Ophelia. Same hair, same figure, same walk. He was two blocks from The Wave, so it was possible.

Wishing the 4Runner stopped, Trace applied the brakes, but far more urgently than Newton's Law allowed for. The vehicle slung sideways. The tires hollered. Trace's collarbone struck the steering wheel and he rolled beneath the dashboard and lay there, stunned. He held a hand to his collar while his heart cannonballed his ears and his brain de-scrambled the scenario: He was still in one piece, unhurt. The car was no longer moving, stalled out. It was morning. Sky looked nice, turning blue, no clouds. Far off, a dog barked. Nearby, a car alarm honked with the urgency of a police siren.

Trace climbed back into the seat and looked through the side window. There she was, standing still, looking at him, stupefied. It was her. Ophelia.

A man emerged from a black Lincoln parked across the street. A few quick strides and the man blocked her way. Trace recognized it was Enrique.

Ophelia saw Enrique too and, though she appeared to know him, she screamed. She ran, but he caught her from behind after only a few steps.

"Hey, hey, hey, why are you running?" he asked her.

Something terrible. To her. Blood dripping. Like something unthinkable. Red and blue rain. Her upside-down face, hair a mop-shaped bundle on the car's ceiling, the perfectly circular pool of blood.

Ophelia tried kicking at Enrique, but this only made her lose balance. "You're hurting me!"

Enrique set his knee on the sidewalk and forced her back

against his other knee. She continued to lash out. "Calm down!" he yelled at her.

Trace sprung out of his car and, within six steps, tackled Enrique off of her. He writhed with him on the ground, his arm hooked around Enrique's throat. Enrique attempted to elbow Trace's ribcage, but he couldn't get the right angle. A jab eventually landed and Trace cried out. He let go and rolled off.

Enrique got partway up in time for Trace to drive a swift, solid shoe into his crotch. It wasn't where Trace was aiming, yet the blow folded Enrique, took him to the sidewalk, chest-first, choking. Trace dragged him to a stand by his hair and forced him against the sidewalk's chain-linked fence, mashing him hard against the fence, making it bend. He pinned his arms behind his back and held them there with one hand. Enrique seemed to be in too much agony to resist.

Trace drew the handcuffs from his jacket and shackled Enrique's wrists. He stepped back and let him fall to the ground where he lay, laboring for oxygen. Trace watched him for a while, then bent over him to dig into his Enrique's front pocket. He found the keys in the other pocket, took the safety deposit key off the ring, slipped it into his own front pocket. Trace dropped the remaining keys near Enrique's knee.

Enrique found his breath. "The hell are you doing, man?"

"Where did you come from?"

"Asshole, uncuff me. You've got them...tight as hell."

Trace concentrated on sobering himself. He strolled to the middle of the empty street. He turned fully to each of the four directions. Ophelia was nowhere to be seen. He cupped his hands around his mouth and called her name, called it until he saw curtains parting in the condominium's stacked windows across the street. Look at me! Every one of you! Open your windows and behold your protector!

He continued calling Ophelia's name, but no use. She was gone.

A gunshot thundered through the morning air. Took Trace only a second to determine its direction: The Wave Hotel.

◆ ◆ ◆

Trace sprinted the rest of the way up the hall. Room 227 was the last door on the left. Finding the door ajar, he went in. The room was dark, so he turned on the light. What he saw took several heartbeats to absorb. There was Drexel, saucer-eyed and pale, holding a small handgun. At his feet, a middle-aged man dressed in black, a large knife protruding from his throat. A dark stain was spreading around his head. Caught in one of those aftershocks which magnify the insignificant, Trace could swear the stain was in the exact shape of North America. Gary Nash lay soaking wet and dead near the wall, his right leg hooked in the open window. A draft pushed the curtains around.

"Um, Drexel," Trace said, his voice quivering several octaves away from its normal pitch.

"I killed him," Drexel said, voice barely there. "I was sleeping, and I woke up because I heard a car alarm, then a gunshot outside, then another beeping noise in the room. Everything was going crazy."

"What happened?"

"The lights were off, but I could see this guy crawling through the window. He had a gun and he fucking shot at me! Blew a hole in the headboard. Dude, I didn't even think. I threw my knife at him."

"Is that his gun you're holding?"

Drexel looked at the weapon in his hand. He put the point of the barrel against his temple. He shut his eyes. "This is it, man. No other way out. I'll go to prison forever now. Maybe get The Chair. I'll never explain my way out of this. Turn around if you don't want to watch."

Trace looked again at the dead man on the floor. Gary Nash's face was calm, no expression whatsoever. To Trace, he looked like any other man lying there, except he was dead with a bowie knife in his throat and important things leaking fluid from his body.

"Hey, Trace. I'm sorry," Drexel said, eyes reopened. "For everything. Like, I know all I've ever cared about was myself, always making sure I had a good time, no matter what. If someone got hurt or I did them wrong, it was their problem. Life wasn't long enough to screw around with, you know? And it seemed like I was always allowed to do whatever I wanted anyway. Look where I've ended up. Standing here with a gun against my head. Dead people everywhere. Guess I've lived a pretty selfish life, haven't I?"

"And you're ending it in a selfish way, too." Trace liked that. It was good. A strong, appropriate reply. He needed more lines like that.

"Even if I don't go to jail, what is there left for me to do?" Drexel looked at the gun in his hand, then replaced its barrel against his temple. "All I'm good for is taking pictures of. No other job skills, but stripping. What kind of future do I have? No thanks. I'm out of here. Trace, I'm giving you one last chance to turn around before I do this."

"You could go to school. Save some money. You can figure something out. Man, don't kill yourself. Think about your friends."

"What friends? You?" After a tremendous deal of shifting and digging, Drexel managed to take something rectangular and silver from his front pocket. He tossed it to Trace. "Here's your tape recorder back."

Trace caught it, looked at it. "Where'd you get this?" he asked. He considered pretending he had no idea what this device could mean to anyone, but for what reason?

"Found it in Ophelia's purse," Drexel said. "That's what was beeping. You made her do it, didn't you?"

"I don't know what to say," Trace said. And it was true. He didn't. His next words came from nowhere. "I was only trying to help...everyone."

"Trying to be the hero," Drexel said flatly. "I get it. You're probably a good cop."

"I'm not a good anything." Trace underhanded the mini-recorder onto the bed. He met Drexel's eyes. "Please, don't kill yourself. What about Ophelia? She's crazy about you."

"Where is she?"

"She left, man. You shouldn't have done that. What you did. It wasn't right. Like, not at all." No, that was a bad thing to say. He needed Drexel to think positive about himself. Or would a stern approach be more effective?

"I shouldn't have done what? Kill this guy? He was going to kill *me*! Holy hell, Trace, I've killed someone else." As if he'd forgotten. Drexel seemed on the verge of tears again. "What in the hell's going on? Ah, God…" He plunged his left hand into his hair and left it there. He began lowering the gun with his right hand but appeared to think better of it. He raised the gun, but dropped both arms, flustered, caught somewhere between resolve and panic.

"I was talking about what you did to Ophelia," Trace said, though he realized her nosebleed was likely from cocaine again, not physical abuse. "Drexel, you practically bashed the poor girl's face in," he added.

"What the hell are you talking about?" Insulted and disbelieving, Drexel relaxed the arm with the gun yet again, but returned it halfway up when Trace dove.

The two of them fell against the bed and slid to the floor. They grappled furiously, Drexel holding his arms straight above his head, trying to elude Trace's reach. But when Trace pressed a knee into Drexel's sternum, it caused him to bend forward, allowing Trace to find a grip on the gun. He refused to let go. From there, it was a strength match, both friends straining to overpower the other. Groaning, Trace put every last bit of energy behind a single vicious yank. The suddenness of the force made Trace kick and his heel struck Drexel's surfboard propped on the wall. The board fell hard onto Drexel and the gun came free from his fingers.

Deflated without a weapon, Drexel offered no further resistance as Trace climbed on top of him, sitting astride his chest. They stayed this way for a minute, winded and numb.

"You...*ha!* You saved my life, you freak," Drexel said.

"You can't help being who you are," Trace blurted. He sat back. He held the pistol, a .32 he noticed. The weapon felt warm and hard and heavy. "Actually, no, you can help it. All I know is that I'm not you, I'm me. And that's fine."

"Know what I've been thinking, man?" Drexel asked. "We should've never even left Atlanta. We had to want more though, didn't we? And we already had everything. What else did we think we needed?"

"Dignity?"

Drexel laughed, but it was cheerless. It was the laughter of someone who'd had their life come unraveled and didn't know what else to do about it. "Yeah, dignity. Good one."

Trace thought over what Drexel had said and had to admit he didn't completely disagree with him. They were in the same room with a powerful man who had met a violent death. They definitely should've never left Atlanta. A father and his daughter would still be alive.

"Anyway," Trace said to his friend. "You're under arrest. I'm sorry."

28

The line outside Rose's Rock Spot consisted mainly of pale teenagers with hairstyles the shape of weaponry, skeletons being the most popular theme among their T-shirts. Screaming, bloody skeletons, skeletons rising out of the ground, skeletons swinging swords and holding shields, skeletons with fangs and bat wings. Death was horrible and it was coming to get you. Yeah!

Trace suggested they go elsewhere for a drink. He wasn't sure why Enrique would even suggest such an establishment in the first place. Ignorance probably.

A few blocks west, they found a bar unfamiliar to either of them, probably unfamiliar to most. An out of the way box in the wall, its outside adorned with cloud-shaped water-stains in overlaying shades, a place calling itself "The Middle Digit." This was what the rectangular sign by the front door informed them along with a hand, its middle finger extended, giving the bird to anyone entering.

Inside, two Budweiser lampshades hung suspended over parallel pool tables, their smooth green fields crisscrossed by cue sticks. The bar reeked of cigarette smoke blended with salt, sweat, despair. The barmaid was a black-pompadoured woman. Her Pink Floyd T-shirt strained against her doughy torso, snug as a condom. Her smile showed missing teeth.

Trace and Enrique both took a stool.

The only people accompanying them at the bar were a man and woman, hip-to-hip on their stools. The man's arm lay around the woman's waist and he whispered into her hair, grinning, anticipating her laughter. He got it.

As Trace heard her laugh, he mused on why he was here. Enrique had called, offering to buy those drinks he owed him for taking the initial O.D. call alone on New Year's Eve. He realized he'd never gotten around to buying them. Promise was a promise.

The first swallow assuaged Trace of any concerns. Didn't matter. He was here. There was beer. He finished half his bottle before noticing he'd done so. He told himself to slow down. Go steady. Do not get annihilated again. No more annihilation.

"So that was intense." Enrique's voice squeaked and he had to cough it clear.

"What were you doing there? You surprised me."

"Keeping a close eye on the man. I was worried he might do something insane and spoil everything."

"Why the secrecy?"

"I could ask you the same thing."

Trace shifted on his stool. "Thanks for not telling on me. By the way."

"Where's the money?"

"I gave it all to Ophelia. It's the arrangement we should've stuck to."

"Oh my God." Enrique shook his head and pried a cigarette pack from his front pocket, dropped it on the bar. He fingered his other pocket for a lighter. "She played you against me."

Trace sagged. "What? Who did?"

Enrique laughed, louder than necessary. "Dumb ass, Ophelia is the girl I've been hooking up with. *She's* my girlfriend."

Trace let this sink in. "Bullshit," he said.

"The entire plan was hers. Everything. Taping her boyfriend was even her idea." Enrique rested an elbow on the bar, the other on the arm of his stool. "I was in love with her, Trace. I would've done anything for her. She used both of us."

"You're fucked in the head. You're making this up."

"I wish. See, her and I were supposed to split the money. Your portion was meant to have you involved, so you'd keep quiet."

Trace hesitated while the moon and sun switched places. "You and Ophelia?"

"Did you sleep with her? Don't lie to me."

"Did *you*?"

"She's the girl I was with on New Year's Eve! When I called you?"

"Wait, but I had to *beg* Ophelia to go through with taping Drexel."

"All an act. It'd be suspicious if she seemed eager, wouldn't it?"

Trace shook his head slow. "Where'd you even meet her?"

"At a club. Around. I have a whole life you don't even know about."

"Apparently. Who the hell are you?"

"A very weak man. Look, she's the one who poisoned Mr. Nash's daughter. She didn't do it on purpose. She meant to poison her boyfriend. She actually came to me after it happened. You understand she's crazy, right?"

"Why would you be in a relationship with her when you know she's also with Drexel?"

"That's the biggest reason I went along with her plan actually. To clear him out of the way."

"Was her relationship with you a coincidence, or she sought you out to do this because you're a cop?"

"It was a coincidence. Or I'm not exactly sure. Now that you mention it."

"Either way, you both made money off Gary Nash from his daughter dying."

Enrique rolled his eyes, surrendered his hands. "*I* didn't! *She* did. You went and gave her all the money."

"I had no idea though. Why didn't you trust me?" Trace believed the sudden tremor against his thigh originated from within his body somehow. A second vibration and he realized it was the buzz of his cellphone there, going off.

He opened his phone, bent back to see the phone number. It was her. He'd called her five times that afternoon. She was calling him back now, though not with the best timing.

"Important call?" Enrique asked.

"I'll take this outside."

"I know it's her. It is, isn't it? Don't pretend it isn't."

Ophelia voice sounded shaken and hurried, barely audible above a riotous symphony of poundings and voices. She'd called him from somewhere very loud and very crowded. He plugged a finger in his other ear and leaned into the wall.

"Is the money in a safe place?" he asked her.

"Safer now, yeah."

"Good." He held his breath a second, waited. "Enrique told me everything. This the part where you disappear on me?"

"I feel bad if I hurt you, Trace."

"I don't feel too wonderful about it either. Guess I got carried away." He waited. She said nothing. "I think I might've even loved you," he said. He listened. "Ophelia?"

She'd already hung up.

As Trace reclaimed his stool, he heard the barmaid saying to Enrique: "And the only reason anyone—the newspapers, the TV—*anyone* gave a damn is because she was a fashion model. If she'd been some female minority from Liberty City, there wouldn't have been one drop of ink spilled or one second of airtime anywhere about any of this." She spoke with her hands planted on the bar, her arms locked straight. "Being breedworthy. That's what it's all about, right? Biology?"

The bar's entrance brightened, went dark again. A shirtless man with a braided beard and wearing an Australian safari hat had joined them. A leashed iguana rode his shoulder, its tail extending nearly to the bearded man's waist.

"But, hell, I was married to a guy for ten years who beat the shit out of me at least twice a day," the barmaid said, which likely explained her missing teeth. "But I stayed with him for years because he was so good-looking and my sisters were jealous. Who am I to talk?" She walked over to where her newest customer sat and kissed him hello. A friend.

"How did *that* start?" Trace asked Enrique.

"I was stretching and she saw my gun. She got bent out of shape, so I had to explain."

"Every detail?"

"Okay, I'm a blabbermouth. I'm a wreck. But she's right. All our other cases swept aside because some billionaire's spoiled, shit-for-brains daughter partied so hard one night that her heart stopped beating. It's messed up."

Trace made Enrique's words a voice over to a cuckoo clock, which sat by the cash register. The clock was birdhouse design, pegged perch, A-framed roof, a bed of plastic branches. The twin doors were stuck ajar, the cuckoo bird gone. Stolen. Or flown away.

The first man left his stool and began a solo game of pool, except he hit the balls directly into the pockets without the aid of a cue ball. Meanwhile, the woman narrated a story to him, which involved her as a life-toughened protagonist, using her harsh wit to put some stupid person in their place.

Enrique asked, "Who called? Was it her?"

"Wrong number."

"I'll bet."

"What are we going to do? Go after her? She did kill someone."

"Bet your ass we're going after her. She's not getting away with this shit."

"A lot of ugly info might come out. About us."

"Fine. I am going to find her. I am going to see her again. I promise you."

"Let's do it then."

From the corner of his eye, Trace watched Enrique look at him, offering him a bemused once over. "I suck," he said. "For going behind your back like that. I got carried away."

"She seems to have that power."

A doppler wave of ambulance sirens blared down the street, stalling right outside but soon continuing. With one finger, the barmaid stroked a scaly, luminescent flap of serrated skin beneath the reptile's chin. It held completely motionless. "My girlfriend," she said to the bar at-large, "she told me how hard these things are to have as pets. Because they're cold-blooded. No matter how much attention, care, and love you give them, they're never going to love you back."

"Your friend doesn't know what the hell she's talking about," the bearded man said in an Australian accent, which explained his Aussie safari hat.

Trace agreed out loud, raising his empty bottle. Hell no, she didn't know what she was talking about. Had she ever *tried* loving a reptile?

29

Luckily none of the other inmates owned even the slightest interest in raping him. Drexel grew accustomed to the concept of jail. A little imagination and he was six years old again, banished to his bedroom for misbehavior; yet, this was a large, concrete bedroom with one wall made of bars and fifty-plus beds and two hundred-plus roommates. Not like a bedroom at all really.

Some hours later, he thought of calling the guard over, so he could tell him, "All right, seriously...Let me out." The realization that he could not do this came as a wet towel slap. He was no longer a free man, no longer trusted with the privilege of making choices. He was a prisoner again. He sat within a patch of sleeping men. He watched a movie on the television set sitting atop a projector stand, situated at the front of the cell. He tried concentrating on the movie's story, forget where he was, but the volume on the TV was shot. It was a dance flick, late-Eighties production, *Dirty Dancing* or something like it. Without sound, the people dancing appeared incredibly foolish.

The noise inside the cell intensified. Or perhaps his tolerance had eroded so his mind paid more attention to it. Over two hundred prisoners laughing, shouting, speaking, coughing, sneezing, snoring, and noise, noise, and more noise, louder and louder. My God! Inmates argued on and over the telephone.

They argued over standing space, blankets, pillows, TV channels, TV shows, shower turns, bathroom turns. Drexel remained as motionless as possible.

A guard came to the bars with a clipboard and shouted a name. A skinny, shirtless kid with a blue mohawk acknowledged him, jogged to the front of the cell, and the guard unlocked the door for him. Apparently, his bail had been met. After being booked, Drexel himself had used his one phone call for a bail bondsman, but the one he chose from the yellow pages had changed numbers. He wasn't allowed to retry.

"Dude dress all fancy. He a pimp? Yo! You a pimp?"

"Pimp? He look like *Gaston*. Hey, Ray-Ray." Raucous laughter, then: "Look him. He look like *Gaston! Beauty and the Beast*, motherfucker!"

Drexel knew without turning that the observations were about him. He prayed for peace. No more fights, please. I've had enough physical confrontations for this life, thanks. He sat in a corner by himself.

A different guard came to the bars and, as before, the inmates stiffened in anticipation, praying for their turn to be bailed. Drexel was no exception. The guard called a name, but it belonged to someone else.

Drexel wouldn't have thought it possible but, after the movie, he grew drowsy. Too many drugs, not enough sleep. Some leftover jetlag, too. Bunching his shirt into a pillow, he lay down, and faded out in seconds. He dreamed of a pitch-dark room, booming with profanity. He dreamed of dead men with knives in their throats.

When he awoke, the caged wall clock above the guard's office said, 1:17.

The guard returned to the bars and called another name. A kid looking barely eighteen strutted out of the cell with his arms raised high, victorious, bailed. The guard shut the cell door, putting the full strength of his arm into it.

Drexel's resolve arrived like the spreading of warm water. He stood and walked to where a collection of men held heated counsel over the jail cell's solitary telephone, a black, nicked-up rotary, decades-old. He saw the situation involved the same dozen men using the phone over and over. One watched the wall clock to time the calls, while another governed whose turn it was. But the correct time and order of turns were a matter of continuous debate.

When Drexel gave notification that he needed to make an important call, it was acknowledged he would have a turn. He half-expected to be ignored, left waiting for hours while the same dozen men kept using the phone, and there would be nothing he could do about it. However, twenty minutes later, he was handed the phone and told he had to dial "9" for an outside line. He dialed his agency and the phone rang for a long time.

A man answered. "K-Oz."

"Evan?"

"This is."

"It's Drexel, man. I'm in jail."

"For what? In Miami?"

"Downtown. Think the agency might spring me? I'll pay it back, every cent. Swear. I'm desperate!"

"What's your charge?"

"I'm not even sure. For the love of God, fetch me out of here. I'll explain everything later."

"How much is your bail?"

"Two hundred thousand."

"What? I can't hear you? Tell those people to stop shouting!"

"My bail is two hundred thousand!"

"Is the interference on your end or mine? I can't hear you! Talk louder!"

"Two! Hundred! Thousand! I need it to get out of here! Please!"

"Drexel, can you call back? Bad connection!"

Evan hung up and Drexel did too. He re-lifted the phone for a second call and ignored the howling protests of the other men waiting: "Naw! You get only one call, man! Get out with that!" He redialed the agency and the phone rang for an even longer time before the answering machine came on. He hung up again with his finger and tried to redial, but a trio of men forced him against the wall until the phone could be wrestled away. Drexel covered his face and stayed pressed against the wall, even after the trio had backed off.

He considered what to do next and not one event felt worth the effort. That was it. Defeat. Struggle extinguished. Drexel sat with his legs straight out before him. He looked at his shoes, which were missing their laces. The lady, the same who'd taken his mugshot and told him his bail, had also made him hand over his belt, his necklace, his earring, and the shoelaces.

At noon sharp, the cell's front door was unlocked and opened. Two different guards sporting buzzed hair, mutton chops, and nightsticks entered and ordered everyone to form a line. For encouragement, the two guards shouted, kicked, and yanked at the prisoners. Like it or not, it was lunchtime. Plastic trays of hotdogs, chips, and coleslaw were passed down the line, followed by cups of water.

Already overwhelmed by sight and sound, Drexel couldn't cope with the additional sense of taste. He gave his lunch to an eraser-haired, gold-toothed youth decked head-to-toe in *Miami Hurricanes* sportswear. He snatched the food without thanking him.

Nearly six o'clock. Another hour and it would be dark outside. It was Drexel's favorite time of day, its end, when the air cooled, the sky held more than one color, the earth appearing softer. There were stars out, but a person could still see things.

Back inside the cell, he saw none of this. He'd returned to the exact spot as before, his back against a bunk leg, his feet straight out. He stared at his shoes some more. Occasionally he would check the wall clock to see if it was tomorrow yet, when he would get to go before a judge. But, no, it was the same sideways day. He couldn't hold up to this. He would have to call his parents. No choice. First he wanted to sit here and soak in his suffering, only until the crowd around the phone lessened. The phone gang had already swelled to thirty members.

The smell, the deafening noise, the lack of freedom, the stigma. Death might've been better. There were even toilets without bathrooms. Two porcelain-bowled receptacles at the back of the cell, standing naked and crusted. He couldn't sit on those, not in front of all these people. Yet, what would he do? Hold it forever?

The guard unlocked the front door of the cell and took a step in. He perched a clipboard against his belly. "Drexel Waters!" he called.

Drexel jumped to his feet. Bailed! What else could it be? He approached the guard, stepping over sleeping bodies the whole way.

"You Drexel?" the guard asked.

"Yes, sir, I am. That's me. I'm Drexel."

"Come this way. Your bail's been met."

He expected Evan or someone else from the agency. Or it was his parents maybe. The agency might have notified them, and they flew straight down. He expected anyone but who it was.

Drexel was led from the cell to the booking room where he signed several forms whose relevance, for the time being, he couldn't care less about. The same lady who had taken his belongings, also gave them back, then pointed him towards a door containing the word EXIT sloppily stencil-sprayed in red paint. After re-lacing his shoes, Drexel thanked the woman. She told him to have a nice day. Be good.

The door had one of those upper-corner air pumps which prevented it from slamming, so the door didn't close behind him, but began to.

She stood a few yards down the sidewalk, swinging a purse against her knee. She stopped when she saw him.

"No way," he said. He hadn't spoken in so long that he sounded strange to himself. "What are you doing here?"

"I paid your bond," Ophelia said. She wore a wrinkled white shirt with green pants, hip-hop baggy. Her eyes were red, bleared. An angry pimple with lesser, satellite pimples erupted at the corner of her mouth. Her frizzed hair escaped its ponytail in every way possible without unraveling it.

"Where'd you get the money?" he asked her. "My bond was a fortune."

"I had some plans come through."

Drexel looked up. The sky was the same as he'd imagined it from inside, except he hadn't given it so much indigo. His eyes followed a bird after it had crossed his line of sight.

"You're welcome," she said.

He laughed, blushing, still watching the bird, though it did nothing more interesting than land on a telephone pole. "I'm speechless," he said. "What you did, getting me out. This is beyond cool. Like, the coolest thing anyone has ever done for me ever."

"I would do anything for you. Guess that's obvious."

"Life with me might get a little disturbing for a while. Can you handle it?"

"Disturb me, yes. It's what I'm doing here." She tucked a strand of hair behind her ear, left the hand on the back of her neck. She studied the ground. "I put something in those drugs I gave you. At the party. It's why that girl died. But it was you I was trying to kill. I tried to kill you."

She started to say more, but he stepped towards her. He placed a hand behind her head and drew her gently towards him. She returned his embrace and, together, they remained that way, wordless, beautiful as a photograph with no one around to take it.

EPILOGUE I

6 MONTHS LATER

Trace watched Enrique dancing with the girl from last night whose name, so she said, was Tuesday. Dance music throbbed to the accompaniment of green light beams and yellow spotlights. At the end of the song, Enrique stopped dancing and cleaned his brow with his forearm. He removed his shirt and tied it around his waist. He shouldered his way off the dance floor, staggering, seeming to wander in the aftermath of a bomb explosion rather than a packed night club.

Tuesday apparently spotted Trace, came over, grabbed his wrists. She pulled him onto the dance floor where he attempted to dance but couldn't get coordinated. Ever since he'd quit stripping, it had become impossible for him to dance without feeling dumb, as if he no longer knew how to dance without shedding clothes in the process. He eventually threw his hands down, begged her off, claimed he didn't like the song. Told her to catch him in a little bit. But don't leave! Trace had left his wallet in her apartment after sleeping with her. This was after she'd given Trace a story about having sex with Drexel. She'd also heard rumors about him and Ophelia hiding in South America somewhere.

Trace watched Enrique as he walked out the front entrance and went left. Where the hell did he think he was going?

Trace considered whether or not to follow him. He didn't want to leave the girl, but she'd already assured him she wasn't going anywhere. Trace decided to make his inquiry quick.

He squirmed his way towards the front, then fast-stepped after Enrique as he passed the broad line of people waiting to get in, many of them haggling with a transvestite doorperson:

"Bro, let us in already. This is ridiculous! We've been waiting over an hour!"

"But my name should be there! You've got the wrong damn guest list."

"You're not listening to me. I know Johnny. He said for me to give his name at the door. You're going to lose your job if you don't let me in!"

Others in line snuck glances at themselves in the club's tubular window; in each face, that flash of sad uncertainty.

Trace followed his partner as he rounded the corner of the building. The next corner, another, into the back alley. Still going! Seriously, where the hell did he think he was going? Enrique eventually halted.

He approached a dumpster and propped its lid open against the alley wall. He continued standing there and did nothing more than look down. Trace walked up beside him and spoke, expecting to startle him, but Enrique didn't flinch.

"Um, what are you doing?" Trace looked into the dumpster with him. The interior was mostly shadowed and what was visible was tinted sodium-orange from the overhanging streetlight. Trace could make out a few plastic garbage bags, some swollen but intact; others split, gushing guts made of empty egg cartons, tomato cans, beer bottles, a brain-shaped network of grape stems. There was an amputated mini-trampoline covered in ketchup.

"I was looking for her," Enrique said.

"In the garbage?"

"Just a dream I had. I'm drunk." Enrique let the dumpster lid drop. It expelled a rank rush of air at them.

Trace cleared his throat. "You're really losing your mind,

huh?"

"Money and women." For a second, Enrique reacted as if someone had splashed acid in his face. He smothered it with his hands. "My wife hates me! She has every right to! I've been such a shitty husband. You should've read the email I sent to her." Next, Enrique did an incredible thing: He wept. "What am I going to do now? Trace, I'm so destroyed."

Trace was shell-shocked. In their six-year partnership, he'd never seen Enrique emotionally vulnerable before, let alone *crying*. He reached over and patted him on the back. He wasn't sure of what else to do.

"Let's leave," Trace said. "We have to keep up with that girl because she has my wallet though."

"Yikes." Enrique cleared his eyes with his sleeves. "Guess I was having a little moment there, huh?" He sniffled. "I'm okay now."

"I'll help you get better," Trace said to him. "I'm here for you, okay?"

"You're Mister Sober now, so you understand things, huh?"

"I just want to help."

"Look! Right on! There's a pizza stand over there. Buy me a slice, Trace. One slice? For your partner? For a friend? How about helping me with that?"

"You've got...below your nose...," Trace flickered his finger beneath his own nose. "Running out...There. All right. A slice of pizza. Whatever you want. Anything else?"

"Yes, let's catch this bitch, okay?"

Trace guided him out of the alley. They ended out on Ocean Drive with the sun coming up. Trace gazed at the pink, purple, and blue strip of neon-framed hotels. A little more light and it would be a true postcard shot. So pretty and colorful. He imagined Ocean Drive incinerated by a hydrogen bomb, the whole street a cumulus curtain of glorious orange flames.

EPILOGUE II

Ophelia's first time was with Drexel's new pop band and a group of long-limbed Peruvian girls the other members had picked up, having lured them back to the hotel with their long hair and talk of impending stardom. Drexel's new name was "Hector." Ophelia hadn't decided on her new name yet. "Ruby" sounded nice.

In Room 222 of *L'Hotel Miaflores*, eleven of them gathered and knelt as if to pray around a rectangular glass coffee table. Skull, the bass player, and a girl with elaborate piercings running from her nose to her earlobes went first, doing the work for each other. Ophelia watched with a mixture of horror and exhilaration as the needle sank into their arms, the plunger filling with pink. She watched as Skull and the girl went slack afterwards, heavy-lidded, vacant.

Ophelia had fled the country with him, pending his manslaughter trial. Rather than face trial, Drexel instead chose to combine their remaining assets and disappear. She settled with him in Lima, Peru, where their dollars would last the longest. They lived now only block away from their private room in The Lima White House Hostel, a converted colonial structure, same as the entire neighborhood.

Drexel tied off her arm with a black, studded belt, the same belt everyone else had used. But a different needle. One of the girls was a *Universidad de Lima* medical student and had brought nearly a dozen.

He held a spoon over the flame of a short, shapeless candle. Within the spoon, a brown powder became a baking brown liquid, which the needle sipped up. She closed her eyes as Drexel took hold of her arm. There was a pinch, then pressure. When she opened her eyes to see why he hadn't taken the needle out, she saw that he had and was already injecting himself.

Outside, a siren went by and she went with it, dragged along in its eddy, escorted down furry, black tunnels of warmth, peace, rebirth. Muscles slipped sleepily over crevices and corners and holes of her skeletal system. Clouds. Angels. Diamonds. Desert. Ocean. Lightning. Mountains. My God! An eagle shrieked.

No, it was the phone ringing. Drexel stood, lost his footing and collapsed against the night table, bringing it with him to the floor. Everyone laughed and the room filled to every corner with the sound, like a thousand people laughing. Once Drexel brought the phone to his ear, he said in a cracked whisper, "Hello?"

Ophelia felt abandoned, adrift, as if she'd blown in from another dimension, a puny leaf pushed along by forces far greater than itself. Except honestly it wasn't random. This scene, these people, this feeling, it was what she'd arranged for herself. A sweet sickness to bathe herself in. It was home.

Skull began making out with two of the girls and soon they were undressing each other. Ophelia became transfixed with them, not because they were having sex, but by the impossible amount of movement involved. When she looked back to Drexel, still on the floor, she saw that he'd closed his eyes and settled his arm across his face. She lay next to him and took his arm. He placed it around her.

She stared at Drexel's profile, admired its pleasant angles and smoothness, the combination of which had destroyed her life.

"I love you," she whispered.

A dreamy smile widened his face. "You do?"

"I love you so much," she said. There was a thin line of stubble, which he'd obviously missed shaving, just below his jawline. She touched it. "Very a lot."

Drexel licked his lips. "Cool," he said.

Someone turned on a reel-to-reel tape of what the band had recorded that day at the studio. The music cradled Ophelia in a gelatinous cushion and when she moved her head, her vision dimmed and wavered, as though reflected from inky lake water.

Skull vomited and the sex turned complicated. He was on his side, propped by an elbow. He retched violently while one of the girls played her lips and tongue over his shoulder, oblivious.

Ophelia could no longer watch, feeling ill enough herself. "Cerebral vasculitis" an English-speaking doctor had called it. There was no telling how long she'd been carrying it. Months possibly. An inflammation of the blood vessels in her brain and spine. She got headaches a lot, seismic migraines which caused her to frequently lose her balance. Dizziness was normal now.

The last thing Ophelia saw before dying was one of the other girls putting lipstick on Drexel. He sat against the wall, one leg folded beneath the other. He stared at his left foot, as though baffled by it. Then, with the concentration of surgeon, the girl made wider and wider circles with the lipstick, caking his entire face with red.

Ophelia drifted into death. She dreamed she was at a theme park called "Ophelia." She climbed a ladder — up, up, up until she reached the lip of space where a water slide, winding in a zigzag path, delivered her back to Earth. The slide ended past the clouds and she tumbled through the sky. She tried catching herself with a tree branch, but it broke like a toothpick, barely there. She plummeted into a clear water brook, deep and blue as Hell itself.

When she awoke, she lay in pitch darkness. Someone was kissing her. She was naked. In the next room, the phone rang two times and stopped.

"I love you, too," the person whispered. It was Drexel. "I could just eat you alive."

CPSIA information can be obtained
at www.ICGtesting.com
Printed in the USA
LVHW090748211119
638021LV00006B/980/P

9 780578 598789